Penguin Crime Fiction

Editor: Julian Symons

Testkill

Ted Dexter, the fo.... .....ex and England cricket captain,
was born in Milan in 1935 and educated at Radley and Jesus
College, Cambridge, where he gained a blue not only in
cricket but also in golf. His outstanding career, which lasted
for ten years, included sixty-two Test Matches, and ended
after he broke a leg in a car accident. As a freelance
journalist he has written for the *Observer* and the *Sunday
Mirror*, as well as being a member of the B.B.C.
commentary team for Test Matches. He is also a qualified
pilot. Ted Dexter is married, with a son and a daughter,
and lives in London.

Clifford Makins was born in 1925 and is a life-long cricket
enthusiast. He was educated at Lincoln Grammar School
and served in the Royal Armoured Corps during the Second
World War. He then worked in the theatre, as stage
manager to the Young Vic Company, and in publishing.
He was editor of *Eagle* from 1959 to 1961, sports editor of
the *Observer* for the next ten years, and since then he has
been working freelance.

Ted Dexter and Clifford Makins

Testkill

Penguin Books

Penguin Books Ltd, Harmondsworth,
Middlesex, England
Penguin Books, 625 Madison Avenue,
New York, New York 10022, U.S.A.
Penguin Books Australia Ltd, Ringwood,
Victoria, Australia
Penguin Books Canada Ltd, 2801 John Street,
Markham, Ontario, Canada L3R 1B4
Penguin Books (N.Z.) Ltd, 182–190 Wairau Road,
Auckland 10, New Zealand

First published by George Allen & Unwin Ltd 1976
Published in Penguin Books 1977
Copyright © Ted Dexter and Clifford Makins, 1976

Made and printed in Great Britain by
Hazell Watson & Viney Ltd
Aylesbury, Bucks
Set in Linotype Pilgrim

Testkill is a work of fiction. The setting of an England v. Australia Test Match at Lord's is of course a real one and the authors are grateful to MCC for allowing the specially printed card of the match to be used in the book. None of the events described, however, has taken place and none of the characters in the novel, even when holding an official position, nor any of the cricketers described as playing in the Test Match are intended as portraits of living persons.

Thursday

Thursday 19 June at ten in the morning. In the old graveyard behind St John's Wood Church the children were
playing on the swings and I sat on a bench watching them.
Traffic was at a standstill and the roads swarmed with
people. It was the first day of the second Test Match between England and Australia at Lord's, hot and humid with
a strong sun lurking behind heavy clouds. The captain who
won the toss would certainly, unless seized by a dangerous
gambling instinct, choose to bat, but with no great cheerfulness.

An old man walked beside the gravestones that line the
far wall, inspecting them closely. In search of dead
cricketers perhaps. His lightweight suit was old and biscuit-
coloured. He wore a straw hat and an MCC tie and field
glasses slung around his neck. He caught my eye and responded with a blink of recognition but we had never been
introduced and he passed me by. I fumbled with the papers,
looking rather than reading, trying to make up my mind
about the chances of The Godmother winning the 3.30 at
Ascot. 'Don't spend the holiday money,' Peggy had said as I
left home and I thought how the usual reproach behind her
smile had lost its affectionate edge since she had discovered
from well-meaning deadly friends the full extent of my
affair with Julia. This was now six months old and, as is so
often the case, showed all those signs of getting both better
and worse at the same time.

My name is Jack Stenton. I captained my county and
played for England. I batted first wicket down and scored
my share of runs at a time when there was a vintage crop

of fast bowlers to cope with. Like some other first-class cricketers I turned to journalism to write a column for a national daily newspaper. My background was comfortable and conventional and at forty-five I am now considered by many to be yet another representative of a dying class. I was a public schoolboy and learned my cricket by a combination of good coaching, good wickets and strong competition. I was a cricket blue, a Rugby blue, a fair sprinter and a top amateur golfer. Those are the sporting facts. My religion is passive Anglican, my wife's active Catholic. We have two daughters at a convent school in Hampstead where we live just off the heath. I once owned a race horse called Italian Style but it never won a race, fell ill and had to be put down.

My father, also a racing and a betting man, was a successful banker who lived to see me make my first century at Lord's in a Test Match. For him that was the true glory. I had reached 80 in 100 minutes but then he could stand no more of it. He prowled behind the pavilion until a great roar went up, then rushed back to the Long Room convinced that the prize had eluded me. He was just in time to see the ball at rest by the pavilion rails. A straight drive from the Nursery End had brought my score to 102. Before my father had time to sit down I smashed the next ball waist high to mid-off who, though tempted to get out of the way, stood his ground and stoically caught it. And my father, turning to an old friend who had witnessed the drama, said, 'What did I tell you, the boy lacks concentration.' He was not too pleased when a former England cricketer standing behind him said exactly the same thing. Poor father, poor mother. They both died last year in the same month, mercifully snatched from a life of increasing incapacity. They had given me love and left me some money. I had taken both for granted. Glancing at The Times I saw that the deaths for the day heavily outnumbered the births and marriages. I got up, disposed of the papers and went for a walk before meeting Julia.

The Rossetti in Ordnance Hill opened its doors sharp at eleven. Julia, punctual as ever, stood at the bar drinking a tomato juice. She prodded my belly with that pointed, insulting attitude of those who never have to worry about their weight, bought me a large pink gin and began talking in the manner of one whose conversation has been briefly interrupted though I had not seen or spoken to her for a week. Her phone had been silent. Where had she been? I cursed the agreement we had made never to question one another's movements.

I have a vivid memory of her that morning. She wore a mauve silk dress that swore triumphantly at her red hair. And there was a dark green suede bag that matched the colour of her eyes. She spoke quickly and precisely, her voice soft and low, an excellent thing in a woman but strangely contradicted by a high ringing laugh that would pierce the din of a cocktail party. She had a nervous, abrasive nature and a very secretive one. That was partly why I knew strangely little about her. She had a reticence about her background that was complemented by my congenital lack of curiosity in the personal lives of other people and her age was apt to vary with her appearance. She could look twenty-five or thirty-five, and any of the years between. She appeared to be of independent means, though there were hints (no more than dark ones) that she was handsomely kept. Certainly she had a magnificent flat near Lord's, in the Abbey Road, gave excellent parties and knew cricket and cricketers. She had spent some time in Australia, the West Indies and France. Her political naïvety and social awareness were overwhelmed by her sexual magnetism. I had never known a woman so much at ease, with or without her clothes.

I am not only a moderate talker but at times can be a very bad listener. I became aware that Julia was talking about the Australian captain Hunt and the dinner she had had with him the previous evening. There have been very few poor captains of Australia and Hunt certainly was not one of them. During his spell as captain he had acquired just enough polish and urbanity to meet the social graces, but essentially he was tough, rough and uncompromising and liked nothing better than to win all games by crushing margins. Especially those against England, and *in* England, and especially the Test Match at Lord's.

Julia touched me again, this time on my forehead.

'Darling, you look hot and bothered. What's the matter?'

'What's that?' I came out of a trance.

'Hunt was saying – now that you're listening – that he always preferred your batting to your writing, but that if you were playing today, at your very old best, they would probably knock your block off.'

'That's nice of him. Let's see who bats first.'

'You talk too much,' she said maliciously, and grabbing my arm in the painful fashion that was so typical of her, pushed me into the short walk to Lord's before play began at 11.30.

This Test Match was to prove a classic, heroic contest. It had its dull patches but the prevailing memory is one of supreme skills, surprise and high drama and rich in those moments when, as the game suddenly changes key and tempo, the onlooker's skin goes cold and the hair bristles. Each day almost 30,000 spectators (television apart) saw the play unfold in an atmosphere of sustained oppressive heat with the special effects of dark cloud, bright sun and thunder and lightning.

Lord's is still reckoned to be the greatest cricket ground in the world. The old Tavern has gone and its replacement is appalling enough; miniature skyscrapers disfigure the horizon as Central London steadily devours the village of St John's Wood, but the ground has retained its sense of proportion and the superb Victorian pavilion (Architect, Mr T. Verity) still subdues all innovations.

I arranged to meet Julia for lunch and left her in the Members and Friends enclosure. The Long Room was crowded and the great windows open against the heat.

This card does not necessarily include the fall of the last wicket

(5p) LORD'S M͞C GROUND (5p)

ENGLAND v. AUSTRALIA

THURS., FRI., SAT., MON. & TUES., JUNE 19, 20, 21, 23 & 24   (5-day Match)

ENGLAND	First Innings	Second Innings
1 W. A. Jarvis.........Warwickshire		
2 P. F. Braunston.Nottinghamshire		
3 D. F. Q. Byron.........Hampshire		
†4 G. Abbott ....Middlesex		
*5 L. Yarcombe ....Kent		
6 A. P. Lyndhurst...............Sussex		
7 J. L. Kirkstead...........Somerset		
8 A. M. Rippon .....Leicestershire		
9 R. C. Ackroyd............Surrey		
10 M. O. Mappleton........Yorkshire		
11 N. I. Standish ....Lancashire		
	B ,l-b ,w ,n-b ,	B ,l-b ,w ,n-b ,
	Total	Total ....

FALL OF THE WICKETS

1—   2—   3—   4—   5—   6—   7—   8—   9—   10—
1—   2—   3—   4—   5—   6—   7—   8—   9—   10—

ANALYSIS OF BOWLING 1st Innings   2nd Innings

Name	O.	M.	R.	W.	Wd.	N-b	O.	M.	R.	W.	Wd.	N-b

AUSTRALIA	First Innings	Second Innings
†1 M. P. Hunt ....Victoria		
2 I. D. Burnett.........S. Australia		
3 M. J. Maitland ...............N.S.W.		
4 R. H. Madden ...............N.S.W.		
5 T. W. Musgrave ...........N.S.W.		
6 P. Lytton ....Queensland		
7 S. G. Fitzgerald......W. Australia		
8 H. D. Eyre ....Victoria		
*9 A. F. Roper ....W. Australia		
10 R. E. Flinders ....Queensland		
11 H. T. Hindmarsh.........N.S.W.		
	B ,l-b ,w ,n-b ,	B ,l-b ,w ,n-b ,
	Total	Total ....

FALL OF THE WICKETS

1—   2—   3—   4—   5—   6—   7—   8—   9—   10—
1—   2—   3—   4—   5—   6—   7—   8—   9—   10—

ANALYSIS OF BOWLING 1st Innings   2nd Innings

Name	O.	M.	R.	W.	Wd.	N-b	O.	M.	R.	W.	Wd.	N-b

Umpires—H. Kite & P. H. Filbert   Scorers—L. Marks & G. E. Roach

† Captain   * Wicket-keeper

Play begins 1st, 2nd, 3rd & 4th days at 11.30 5th day at 11

Stumps drawn 1st, 2nd, 3rd & 4th days at 6.30 5th day at 5.30 or 6

Luncheon Interval 1.30—2.10

Tea Interval 4.15—4.35 (may be varied according to state of game)

England had won the toss and elected to bat. The England captain, George Abbott, was no man for heroics. The umpires, Kite and Filbert, were already nearing the middle with the Australians in pursuit. That distinguished Australian cricketer and journalist, Jack Fingleton, once wrote an incisive piece about his fellow-countrymen, 'The Men in the Baggy Green Caps'. And here they were again at Lord's, baggy green caps and all. They looked tough and jaunty and with one strange exception that caught my eye (the fast bowler, Fitzgerald), were jumping up and down, bursting with spirit and fitness. An exhilarating sight but one, I must confess, that tended to get on my nerves.

There was time for another look at the scorecard. There was very little form to go on. From the start of the tour the weather had been bad, but the crux of the series was whether the ageing England side, holders of the Ashes, would be able to hang on to them in the face of the Australian fast-bowling threat and the three up-and-coming batsmen from New South Wales.

Whenever I look back at that first day's play, with the scorecard in my hand, I feel again that childish futile obsession with time and place, in perfect step together, just like Jarvis and Branston walking down the pavilion steps and through the gate and onto the field. Would all this have happened had I not been there? Yes, yes, of course it would. The buzz of anticipation that lasted until the batsmen reached the wicket subsided into chatter as Jarvis took guard and awaited the first ball from the Nursery End. Then, as the Australian field settled down, silence, while Hindmarsh, after pacing out his run, turned and stopped for a second.

Outside my own country I have played Test cricket in Australia, New Zealand, India, Pakistan, the West Indies and South Africa. Nowhere, not on any ground, have I experienced the thrill, the inward thump that occurs before the first ball is bowled on the first morning of a Test at Lord's between England and Australia. And on this morning there was something extra. The Australian fast attack was in the hands of two men who were born killers of first-, second- and third-class batsmen. Neither had played in the First Test at Trent Bridge – a draw and ruined by rain. It was a strange situation. Until now Hindmarsh and Fitzgerald had not played together, neither in the few county matches nor against the MCC side at Lord's. That game, which Hunt had not captained (he had a sore throat and a high temperature), had been a subdued affair (and another draw) with Fitzgerald absent and Hindmarsh reluctant to let himself go. Yet against the counties, first Hindmarsh and then, especially, Fitzgerald had revealed in short, devastating spells an alarming hostility that had not only destroyed the confidence of county batsmen but had aroused anger and disapproval in the cricketing press, both provincial and national.

There was a feeling that the fast-bowling controversy, as old as the hills, was now operating, in the persons of these two Australians, in a new, virulent strain with a very grave threat to life and limb. Their absence at Nottingham was greeted with bewilderment and suspicion. Hindmarsh, it was announced, had a back strain and Fitzgerald a heavy cold. It may have been the truth. Both players were non-committal, although it was observed that Fitzgerald had not even the trace of a sniffle. Some said quietly that his character and disposition were as much a worry to his own side as to his opponents.

The sun had not broken through, the atmosphere was heavy but the light quite good. There was little grass on the pitch. Earlier in the season, following a wet winter, county pitches had little substance to them and took spin early on. The maxim was, win the toss, bat first and win the match. But you never can tell. The head groundsman, Merryweather, had suffered enough from his name to learn to suffer fools gladly, especially those who asked him what kind of pitch he had prepared for a five-day Test Match. 'It will be hard and fast, sir,' he would say, looking amiably in the direction of the pavilion.

Hindmarsh, muscular and compact, bowled into a predictably hostile field with the wicket-keeper standing back. His first delivery was short of a length, wide on the off and fast by any standards. Jarvis left it alone. Hindmarsh continued briskly in his search for line and length and it seemed that even without his consent the ball was moving about in the heavy atmosphere. Jarvis looked slightly ill at ease. No runs came from the over. Jarvis had been playing for Warwickshire since the age of seventeen. After a brilliant start the bowlers had tamed him for the next three seasons. Regaining confidence, Jarvis had made some big scores in key matches and now seemed the best choice as an England opener to partner Branston.

Hunt threw the ball to Fitzgerald who promptly dropped it. Picking it up suggested effort and he seemed in no hurry to begin his stint from the pavilion end. Fitzgerald was a little over medium height, stooping slightly and with very long arms. His run was shorter than Hindmarsh's and he looked awkward until he got into his run, revealing then the classic, contained, highly disciplined style of a first-class athlete. Fast and left-handed, he bowled to the left-handed Branston who took an easy single off a thick edge down to third man and when the field changed over Jarvis got off the mark in the same way. Then Hindmarsh pushed on with his second over. The Australian bowlers were respecting the English tradition, pitching the new ball up to the batsmen, even though this was not their style. Then Hindmarsh to Jarvis who, still a little uncertain, managed a streaky single off the last ball, bringing him to face Fitzgerald who, nodding his head as in approval of the thickening light, proceeded to bowl a ten-ball over.

The first three balls, all no-balls, were loudly called by umpire Kite who, though a mild enough character, had an officious style of law enforcement on the field. Umpires, unlike captains, can never hope to win, and as they get older it must be admitted that their thankless task is apt to prey on their nerves. Fitzgerald looked Kite up and down after the third call. For the sake of peace and quiet it was just as well, I thought, that Jarvis had made no effort to play at and possibly score off those three no-balls. The fourth ball was taken direct at third slip, a grotesque wide.

The crowd buzzed and a man standing behind me sniffed loudly. There was a tap on my shoulder. It was the MCC President, Philip Brooke-Stanley.

'See you later on, perhaps,' he said. And with a nod and a grimace he continued on his way to the Committee Room.

Meanwhile Kite was off on another tack, treading down Fitzgerald's footmarks on the follow-through. He said nothing but glanced pointedly in Fitzgerald's direction. Fitzgerald just as pointedly ignored him. I picked up my binoculars to have a closer look at Fitzgerald. They were very powerful glasses, more suited to the race course than the cricket field, and I detected the tell-tale signs of a slight flush seeping into Fitzgerald's deadpan features as he walked very, very slowly to cover for a word with his captain, Hunt. Play resumed and Fitzgerald bowled his six remaining balls to Jarvis. The over had yielded four extras but there were no scoring strokes. Fitzgerald strolled away in an absent-minded fashion. It was a curious business.

Now there was tension in the air. It seemed to affect Hindmarsh by way of a much more hostile over to Branston. This batsman, renowned for his elegant stroke play, decided sensibly to play a defensive, watchful brief. He was forced onto the back foot but managed to keep the ball out. Again no runs.

When Fitzgerald took the ball again there were a few raucous shouts but nobody laughed and the bad light that stops play was in the offing. There was a distant growl of thunder and a further delay as Jarvis asked for the sliding sightscreen to be moved. I took the chance to leave the Long Room and squeezed in out front, behind the bowler's arm. I spotted Julia, sitting away to my right and managed to catch her eye. She removed the Black Russian cigarette from her mouth before drawing a hand across her throat. My wife

Peggy might have crossed herself. Fitzgerald gave Kite an ominous nod and walked back a little beyond his mark. Jarvis tugged at the peak of his cap, a touch of Len Hutton perhaps, and never took his eyes off the bowler. A mistake, I thought. It depends of course on the kind of person, or batsman, you are, but I never, but never, followed the progress of a fast bowler on his walk back. I kept my eye off him until the very moment he came into my sights, near the end of the plunging run. Beware the hypnotic trance, it can paralyse. Fitzgerald tapped his forehead as if recalling some forgotten art, and I realized the full meaning of Julia's gesture. I had been here before. Fitzgerald on the surface was a quiet, dull man, a moderate drinker but with a terrible temper when provoked. He had great success with women and I had seen him throw a man downstairs, breaking his leg and collar-bone into the bargain, and all because a dear, boozy old chap had put his hand up the skirt of a girl at a party she was giving. The incident was hushed up but I still remember the stinging clout she gave Fitzgerald, the mark on his cheek, and his indifference and contempt. The party was Julia's and it was her skirt.

I doubt if Jarvis ever saw the next ball. Certainly, if he moved at all it was in the direction of square leg. The ball struck him about the heart and he folded, dropped his bat and sank to his knees. Fitzgerald turned away and looked at the pavilion. There was shouting and whistling, especially from the ill-informed and those badly placed to see the incident. There was a huddle around Jarvis and the members sitting near me rustled with concern. Then Jarvis emerged, rubbing his heart, hobbling a bit, but waving his arm and asking for his bat and his cap. These were restored to him and a great cheer went up as he resumed his stance. It looked a shaky one to me. Like a man who falls badly he had probably got up too soon, but then he was a stubborn man. Fitzgerald's next ball lifted sharply, flicked a glove or bat handle and shot over the slips for four. There was little to cheer about but we had cheers just the same. Four more balls, all short and aimed to hurt, with Jarvis playing and missing and narrowly surviving. Fitzgerald ambled off to third man and Branston faced Hindmarsh again.

Every batsman, in the eyes of other players, has a courage quotient. For a batsman at a critical moment apprehension, even fear, is often allayed by familiar surroundings, and even the normal chatter of the slips may put him at ease. Branston sensibly took his time, observing forward short leg coming closer, and the placing of another man to add to the crowd in the slips. There was a slight commotion at the Nursery End and the batsman waited patiently for it to stop. A short ball from Hindmarsh was on the cards. In fact he bowled three and Branston swayed out of the way with immaculate evasion. To the fourth ball he played back, a beautiful stroke, but the ball was through him and carried the middle stump towards the wicket-keeper. Branston looked back almost approvingly and made as if to play the stroke again. Fortunately he thought better of it. That was enough elegance for one innings and he walked firmly away.

First wicket down, of course, was Byron. He was tall, blond and handsome and beautifully turned out. In some ways he reminded me of me, the public schoolboy who plays for his university, then a southern county, then England – all inside four years. His temperament was superb and seemed to embody the ideal type described by Sir Donald Bradman. It is the type 'that usually possesses a high degree of nervous energy which comes into play at the critical hour ... He may be anxious on the morning of the match, but once he sets foot on the arena he is in full command of himself and his reflexes are quick ... He is the chap for the big occasion.' Byron, like all great athletes, created the illusion of having more time than others to make up his mind before the moment of decision. He was certainly the finest English batsman of his generation and the crowds flocked to see him. He mostly got out when he was bored, it seemed, rather than from technical incompetence or lack of concentration. Of course, like the rest of us, he was vulnerable to that perfect, unplayable ball that 'pitches on the leg stump and hits the top of the off' (an old dressing room joke). Jarvis, looking composed now, met him at the crease and a few words were exchanged. Byron took guard, examined the field of uncompromising hostility and played out the remaining two balls of Hindmarsh's over, making it look comparatively easy.

Jarvis, still facing Fitzgerald, came down just in time on a nasty yorker and fended the next ball off his chest wide of long leg. His running between the wickets looked clumsy to me but he bravely came back for the second run to keep the strike. Fitzgerald looked pale now and appeared to be muttering to himself. His fifth ball was one of those 'perfect, unplayable' ones but just before the off stump left the ground the echo of Kite's shout of 'no-ball' was heard. Fitzgerald, on the point of mouthing an obscenity, checked himself. In the end he gave the umpire only a perfunctory glance and walked back, looking almost cheerful. He had good cause to be confident. Both he and I and Jarvis knew that the cumulative effect of the sustained hostility was beginning to make its mark. His last ball was lost to me but I heard the emphatic snick and the confident shout and Jarvis was out, caught behind.

Abbott, the England captain, was a specialist batsman, an acknowledged master of English conditions. But then he played well anywhere. He was enormously popular at all county grounds and as a Test Match captain was utterly just, encouraging even to those members of the side he might not have picked himself. The crowd rose to him and he touched his cap in salute. Abbott was never without his cap, though he might well have been glad to be without Fitzgerald and Hindmarsh at this moment of the game. That morning at Lord's, under a thick sky and in the clinging heat, was not the best time to cope with fast bowling of such quality and menace. Byron, motionless, rested on his bat like a master waiting yet another disciple. Then as Abbott's broad beam neared the crease he moved forward to greet his captain. A few brisk nods, some brief gestures and Byron was facing Hindmarsh again. Another ripple of thunder hinted that the game might be utterly changed by a vicious downpour, bringing rain upon the just and the unjust alike. I went back to the Long Room.

Byron cut Hindmarsh past third man who never moved, then left Hunt rooted in the covers. Perhaps we should enjoy the cricket after all. Fitzgerald began to bowl to Abbott. This was the crunch. If Abbott went quickly then the England innings would be seriously damaged, perhaps irrevocably. I couldn't think of a better player than Abbott to sit it out and then slowly to build a considerable, if dogged, score that would give the innings stability. The fast attack with the new ball was still full of energy but it must flag before too long. It was essential to see off the speed merchants and hope to gain a breathing space. But then, in four balls only, Fitzgerald set the haystack on fire. The first struck Abbott on the pad and the thump was drowned by the bowler's appeal. Kite was unmoved and walked on the pitch again looking at Fitzgerald's marks. Abbott played and missed at the second which shaved the off stump. He nudged the third, not too surely, down to third man, and might have been glad of a single only, but Byron was running like a hare and Abbott was back with Fitzgerald again.

It is one of the compensations of batting at the highest level that the totally random element of selection ball by ball is, to some extent, mitigated by a state of exceptional awareness. Very often a Test batsman in form can anticipate, quite accurately, what a great bowler will do next. Abbott was, however, in no such condition at this moment and was facing a man who was, at best, a most unpredictable customer. His senses would have told him only that Fitzgerald was now operating at peak effort when an extra yard of pace can be generated without perceptible increase in muscle power. Any golfer will have memories of a particular drive which flew, say, thirty yards further than the rest, a huge increase in velocity being achieved simply by balance, co-ordination and timing. Fitzgerald's fourth ball had just such a freak quality.

Abbott, playing back instinctively, was wrong-footed, bat adrift in his hands, and he took it straight between the eyes. He seemed to consider the consequences for a second, then fell to the grass. There was no sign of life, no movement at all, and after the silence a great gasp of dismay cut through the heat. There was little delay. Whatever had happened to Abbott it was decided to move him quickly and he was carried from the field. They came up the steps and I saw the blood seeping through a handkerchief over the man's face. Fitzgerald, aloof, stood with hands on hips yet without the slightest trace of triumph or defiance. He was as pale as ever and stood like a statue under the dark sky.

Indignant murmurs, boos and shouts of anger came from the seats at the Nursery End. A black man shook his fist from where the Tavern used to be. Stewards and police appeared on the grass by the boundary. Mr Merryweather and his men walked on the field looking watchful and protective.

I turned to look at my neighbours and saw the President nimbly weaving his way towards me.

'Well,' said Brooke-Stanley, 'this seems as good a time as any. Can you spare a moment?'

There was a bitter smile on his thin, sharp face. He wore it permanently, shiny and very well-pressed like his suit. 'Come along to the back,' he said. And we made our way to the rear of the pavilion and stopped by a dusty door that looked like the entrance to a broom cupboard. That in fact had been its original function but the President had commandeered it for his personal use on special occasions. The President's own man, Francis, stood there waiting.

'Good morning, gentlemen,' said Francis, opening the door. 'It is gone noon,' said the President and we went in.

There were some hard chairs and a table with bottles, glasses and ice in a plastic bucket. Brooke-Stanley made large pink gins then sat down, staring at the dusty ceiling. He was well into his seventies and you could only call him well-preserved but the eyes were remote and the hands shook slightly and he gave the impression of having suffered long enough. Long ago he had captained England as an amateur and was remembered as an indifferent but enthusiastic player with a passion for bowling fast. There had been business interests in London and Sydney, a long spell in a Japanese prisoner-of-war camp, and various positions of power and influence in MCC where he still managed a say in the selection of Test sides. He was also an old friend of my father's and when as a young batsman I was described by the cricket writer, Festing, as 'having all the great qualities apart from that of staying in', Brooke-Stanley declared his faith in me and would not budge. Certainly I had owed my main chance to him and had grown fonder of him as we both grew older. He was a curious old fellow and very well informed about my private life.

'I'm worried about Fitzgerald,' he said at last.

'Who isn't? I wouldn't have fancied him much under these conditions. And he has a very mean streak.'

'Just so,' said Brooke-Stanley peering into his glass. 'Do sit down for a moment.'

He was still looking into his glass as if it contained a picture or a message that he wished to describe or relate to me. I was puzzled. It seemed an odd time for a drink and a chat. Was he worried about his personal life, or mine, or Julia's? He knew about the affair but had never seen fit to admonish me about it. Though often brusque and off-hand in his dealings with people, I had always put this down to shyness. There was a patient and kindly streak in him if only you could detect it.

I didn't sit down but said, 'I really should find out what's going on. The office will be on to me. It's always the same when a man gets laid out.'

He swallowed some gin and said, 'He may be possessed by fear.'

'Who, George Abbott?' I started drinking now. 'No. Never.'

'I was thinking of Fitzgerald,' he said, now looking straight at me.

'Fear, fear?' I repeated the word as if its true meaning had always eluded me. 'I don't follow you.'

'He has been warned,' said the President.

I thought of Kite. Perhaps the umpire had had a firm exchange with Fitzgerald that I had failed to notice.

Suddenly the President's eyes showed the awareness of a misunderstanding.

'Threatened,' he said. 'Threatened might be a better word. Fitzgerald has been threatened with his life.'

The noise of the crowd, not a roar but a very loud murmur, came through the closed door. The President stood up.

'Time to get back,' he pronounced, as if I'd been wasting his time and our encounter had been a silly mistake.

'But —'

'We'll talk about it later. You'll keep quiet, of course.' And he swept past me and out of the door. This wasn't good enough, I decided quickly, and went after him. I nearly knocked him down for he stopped quite suddenly. His long fingers bit into my arm.

'Come back for a moment,' he whispered, none too quietly, and at once we were back in the room with the hard chairs and the hard liquor.

'You haven't finished your drink,' he said, pouring me another one.

I controlled an impulse to burst out laughing and said, 'Are you feeling all right?'

'No,' he replied sharply, 'I'm not.'

'Why don't you go home for a while?' I said fatuously, though it was a practical suggestion. The President had a house in Elm Tree Road just beyond the ground and could enter through a little door let into a pair of big gates that were permanently bolted and barred. Little doors! Shades of Alice in Wonderland. Perhaps the old man had suddenly gone as mad as a hatter.

'It was at Nottingham, you see,' he said briskly. I didn't see at all, but then he went on, 'As you know, Fitzgerald wasn't playing in the First Test. He was unfit – bad cold, that sort of thing.'

Now I was curious. 'How bad was the cold?'

'Never noticed it myself. Not on the Monday anyway – that's when I had a drink with him, you know.'

I tried a patient but firm approach. 'Now then. You keep saying "you see" and "you know", but at the moment I don't see or know anything at all. To begin with I wasn't aware that you were at Nottingham.'

'Oh, that was just for the Monday,' he said. 'Spent most of the day with Warsop.'

Warsop was a very old cricketer indeed. All his family were dead and he was almost blind.

'Well,' the President continued. 'There was all that rain and Warsop went home early. Then I met Fitzgerald who said he'd like a word with me. So we had a drink together.'

It sounded a strange encounter but then the most unlikely characters come together at cricket matches.

'Is he a friend of yours?' I asked rudely.

'No,' he replied evenly. 'No, I wouldn't say that. I know a bit about him, of course.'

There was a long pause and I made no effort to cut it short. The President looked absent-minded and I had the impression that he had lost the thread to his thinking. Then he said, 'He was very depressed and morose, and then he told me about this ... er ... threat. I had to laugh. It sounded more a prank than a threat, a silly tiresome thing. But then I wasn't so sure ... there was something else ...'

There was a brisk knock at the door and for one wild moment I expected Fitzgerald to appear and clear up the matter. But it was the MCC Secretary, Peter Forester, an elegant man with long, wavy hair, and one of my contemporaries.

'Excuse me. Oh good grief, drowning your sorrows already?'

'By no means.' Brooke-Stanley switched on his bleak smile.

Forester responded cheerfully. 'Abbott's going for an X-ray. He's a bit dazed and bloody, but Ralph's had a look at him and thinks there's no great damage or danger. But he won't be back today – that's for sure.'

Ralph Stiell, cricket enthusiast and MCC member, was a doctor with a fashionable practice in Devonshire Street. We had never got on.

'Thank you,' said the President, nodding to Forester. 'Do have a drink if you need one.' And he left us without another word.

Forester, like an old-fashioned stake villain, stroked the moustache he was cultivating. 'It looks like being a rough old game,' he said.

'That's right,' I replied. 'And I'd better get back to it.'

Byron had been joined by the England wicket-keeper, Yarcombe, the best since Godfrey Evans, and a fine attacking batsman, not exceptionally graceful but exceedingly nimble and flexible. He was tireless and lived only for cricket. He had matured early and was now in his prime. At the moment he was spared Fitzgerald and Hindmarsh, for both had been finally taken off and succeeded by the seam bowler, Eyre, and Flinders, an outstanding practitioner of the declining art of leg-spin.

There was a lull, the tension eased and by 1.15 Byron and Yarcombe had added 31 runs. The England total, including extras, was 55 for the loss of Jarvis and Branston, with Abbot retired, hurt. I heard a comment that Hunt had let England off the hook, but I wasn't so sure. The light improved slightly and there was movement in the crowd with lunch in mind when Hunt brought back Fitzgerald to replace Flinders at the Nursery End. A complete change of pace. Fitzgerald, ferocity unabated, beat Byron twice then surprised him, almost fatally, with a full toss that rattled the bat, followed by an absurdly short ball that made Roper jump like a goalkeeper to save four certain byes. At the other end Yarcombe played Eyre with confidence. There seemed two easy runs when he pushed a ball wide of mid-on but Byron appeared to stumble and Yarcombe sensibly settled for one. That left him facing Fitzgerald for what turned out to be the last over before lunch.

Hunt put the pressure on, bringing up third man and providing a suicidal silly mid-on. Fitzgerald dawdled, ran up, changed his mind and broke off. He did this a second time, virtually on the point of delivery. It was all very irritating and provoking. The crowd joined in again and Yarcombe lifted his bat and stood aside. When it was quiet, and Yarcombe was back on guard, Fitzgerald threw the ball high above his head, fumbled it, or pretended to, then set off on his run. On he came, rocking slightly but very controlled and confined like an express train rushing through a tunnel. It was the fastest and deadliest of balls kicking up into Yarcombe's face. The batsman, correct and courageous, got his bat in the way and the ball cracked against its face, then, tamed by the impact, rose in a gentle arc to drop sweetly into the hands of Musgrave in the gully.

'Oh dear, oh dear, oh dear.'

I turned. It was Mooles, the oldest pavilion attendant in the world, having deserted his post at the door, as was his custom when the cricket got a grip on him.

'Ah Mooles,' I said grandly. 'Now that was a very special delivery.'

'Indeed sir, and what would you have done with it?'

'Accepted it, Mooles, with dignity, I trust, just like Mr Yarcombe.'

'Just so, sir. I look forward to reading you.'

Mooles shuffled off and I closed my eyes. The image of Fitzgerald seemed even brighter in the dark while the crowd noises swarmed like bees in my ears. It was time the day slowed down a little. There was a lot of it left and already its events were on top of me. Slightly dizzy, I opened my eyes to see Lyndhurst passing Yarcombe on his way to the crease. Like Abbott, the vice-captain Kirkstead had steady nerves and would not, at this stage, juggle with the batting order. From the Mound Stand a voice enquired if Lyndhurst had his survival kit handy. The theme was developed and there were cries of danger money. Fitzgerald now went for his man, running in even faster than before, but the extra effort unbalanced him and, unbelievably, Lyndhurst escaped without having to play at a single ball. The players came in to lunch.

Julia was waiting behind the pavilion and talking to a blonde girl in a black straw hat with a pink rose on the ribbon. Polly Parsons was a buxom and curvaceous woman of twenty-two. Her shape was firm and excellent and her clothes, like Julia's, expensive and in very good taste. And there was a touch of vulgarity about her that seemed, on first acquaintance, rather endearing. She had appeared on the cricket scene at the beginning of the season and recently had seen a lot of Julia. She had stayed at the Abbey Road flat occasionally, having no permanent place of her own in London. She had a liking for expensive hotels, restaurants and night clubs. There was a hint of the Midlands in her voice and indeed her home was in or near Birmingham where her father was a property developer. There had been a divorce long ago and her mother had left the country and married a university professor in Strasbourg. I stared at her splendid breasts and Julia, grinding out the remains of another Black Russian, wagged her finger at me. Her eyes were bright and there was a glint of malice in them.

'Now it's rude to stare!'

'I was thinking of something else,' I said boldy.

'Lunch perhaps. Can we sneak Polly in with us? She's made a mess of her arrangements.'

'No need. Here are the tickets. You take her in. I really must go to the Press box. You don't mind?'

'Not at all, darling. You must have a lot on your mind.'

'What about afterwards?'

'Just come round whenever you like. Or go home if you must. Please yourself, you always do.'

I did no such thing but I smiled graciously, touched the rose on Polly's hat and felt the bite of Julia's nails in my palm as I handed her the tickets for lunch.

If you look down through the window of the Press bar at the back of the Warner Stand you can see the back gardens of the houses in Elm Tree Road. A round iron table painted white with graceful chairs to match dominated Brooke-Stanley's small, beautifully trimmed lawn. I had sat there many times talking to him and his guests. Julia was there often and I remember the time when she accused me (she was a born accuser) of staring at her legs, then dumped her escort and invited me back to her flat. That was how it all began. But today the scene was deserted. I suddenly realized that I must see the President again. But better avoid him until the day was done.

In the bar my Sports Editor, Williamson, was drinking with Reginald Festing, the doyen of English cricket writers. He was a bad-tempered man but not without a certain sardonic gusto that appealed to me.

'Ha! The last representative of the Golden Age of cricket. What idiot wrote that, by the way?'

'He's standing behind you,' I said, nodding to Ransley whose youth and eagerness had sustained him well into middle age.

'As for Willie here,' said Festing, 'he really is the most awful pain in the neck. Knows nothing about the game.'

'Oh, do shut up, Reg,' said Williamson good-naturedly. 'Jack, what'll you have?'

'A small pink gin.'

Williamson pushed towards the bar and Festing assumed one of his more agreeable expressions. He was not very popular with the younger writers who discerned, quite correctly, that his experience and judgement and his gift of reading the game had become clouded with bitterness. He was sixty-three and sometimes looked eighty. He had been in the game too long. Soon he would retire but we would never see the last of him. He had been 'wrong' perhaps about me but when I was first selected to play for England he sent me the warmest of good wishes, changed his tune a little ('You know, you'll never be *really* great. I don't quite know why, but there it is . . .'), and when I took up journalism he took me in hand and taught me how to write within my limitations ('Now, none of that Cardus stuff. I never thought him all that good and I can do without any more of his pieces, especially when they are written by someone else.') And more in the same vein. He had been all right, they said, until his wife had been killed in an awful car smash. But he never mentioned it. Sometimes we had lunch or dinner together when he could be an excellent companion.

'Well, Jack, we won't win this one.'

'You know what the man said –'

'Yes, cricket's a funny game, but not all that daft. You'll have to remove Fitzgerald to get away with it.'

Willie, battered from the bar and spilling our drinks, said, 'We'll need 800 words by seven o'clock. And you will talk to Fitzgerald?'

'I'm not sure,' I replied, smiling at Festing and feeling very odd inside.

'Come off it. Do you know, there hasn't been one decent piece on the man.'

'It depends what you mean by decent.' Festing's tone was mild, a sure prelude to one of his irascible outbursts. 'If you can call a hostile, cunning and dangerous man decent, okay. He has a superb action, I'll grant you that, and near-perfect control but his target is never the wicket, it is only and always the batsman, number one or number eleven, it's all the same to him.'

'Now then,' I protested, 'you can do better than that. What the hell does it matter who's batting and in what position. Balls to the fast bowlers' union. Get them out without delay and then score more than they did. That's the name of the game.'

'So you say!' Festing retorted hotly but not without

28

pleasure as he warmed to his theme. 'The name of this game is murder if it goes on like this. I tell you that if Fitzgerald and Hindmarsh (he's almost as bad) – all these Australians are the same underneath, they're as rough as sore arses – if these two aren't checked now, and in this game, if they're not warned, publicly cautioned, and called for dangerous, intimidating play, if they're not stopped, they'll stop the game for good as a contest of skill and grace and endurance. Yes, they'll wreck the whole bloody show.'

Then Thirtle butted in. He was bald and young and had captained Eton, or was it Harrow?

'It was Eton,' he said reading the doubt in my eye. 'Tell me, do you think Fitzgerald is throwing the odd one?'

'More like throwing a fit,' said Festing rudely. 'Jack, are you having lunch?'

'No thanks. I must have a word with Willie.'

'Hard lines. Well, cheerio then.'

Willie and I left the bar to sit in the Press box where the obliging Thirtle produced sandwiches from a very old canvas bag that bore his initials, T.N.T. There was some journalistic chat about bylines, headlines and deadlines, and some idle speculation on the weather, the wicket, the mysteries of cricket and the shifting fortunes of the five-day game. Around me I kept on hearing the name Fitzgerald sounding on and off, the audible equivalent of a flashing light. Meanwhile the light in the sky had steadily improved and when play started after lunch the sun was trying to break through again.

Hunt's handling of his attack seemed a little odd. He ignored Hindmarsh and withdrew Fitzgerald fairly quickly. I wondered whether he had the side fully in his grasp or whether his personal hostility to Fitzgerald was affecting his judgement. However it may have been, within half an hour Flinders was brought back to partner Eyre and they stayed together until nearly four o'clock. And so did Byron and Lyndhurst. It was slow going but the change of the tempo of the game seemed just right. There was little in the wicket for Flinders but he had a masterly session, keeping the ball well up to the bat and proving very difficult to get away. Eyre got some movement now and then, also nagging away, but the England pair supplied the necessary vigilance. Lyndhurst as usual looked awfully dull but at least he stayed in. To my mind he was one of those cricketers beloved of selectors for his great potential. It seemed a long time coming. He had little backlift and rarely played forward. He stayed in his crease, fussing, shuffling and pottering about like a cautious gardener in the plot outside his kitchen door. They made 75 in 105 minutes with Byron reaching his fifty off Flinders' one bad lapse of the afternoon with a precise but cheerful smite for six to mid-wicket.

Willie had returned to the office and Festing sat by me. He was still sipping whisky and water and had put his pipe on. I thought how very well his Royal Yacht would go with Julia's Black Russians and was about to tell him so when he announced that in the next over Hunt would bring back Fitzgerald. He was right. And Hunt added Hindmarsh for good measure. It seems obvious now that Lyndhurst was ripe for the kill. He had been there long enough to feel secure in a little world of his own and looked almost resentful when Roper and his ring of slips appeared behind him, standing well back. There was twenty minutes to tea.

Fitzgerald from the Nursery End bowled to Lyndhurst three balls of increasing violence, each one progressively faster as stiff muscles warmed to their task. Again, the fourth ball was that express delivery expected by all, including Lyndhurst perhaps. He was retreating even before the ball pitched and the issue was decided once and for all when he trod sharply on his wicket. It was a shambles and he shook his hand at the sight, but this I gathered later was more in pain than in anger. The ball had struck him severely on the glove. Festing spluttered furiously as his pipe smoke swirled in his lungs, then swore most obscenely and made a note in a child's exercise book. Lyndhurst retired to scattered applause and in came one of my favourite cricketers.

Kirkstead of Somerset, at thirty-nine, was by far the oldest man playing in this match. He was a tough, outspoken man respected by players but not highly regarded by selectors. I knew it was because of Abbott's insistence that he was playing today. But he bore no grudges and his class and calibre were beyond question. He was a little slower on his feet these days but he had all the strokes and knew when to play them. As a bowler he had been known for years as the poor man's Alec Bedser but this wasn't such a bad mark. He was barrel-chested and had hands like shovels. His eyesight was still phenomenal. He always saw the ball early and to confirm this took 8 runs off the last two balls of Fitzgerald's over – with a delicate glance to the long leg boundary and a thunderous cover drive that caught Hunt literally on the hop. Then in the last over before tea Byron was cornered, one might say, by Fitzgerald who bowled very fast and very short at him. Byron stood up well, or rather ducked and weaved, managing a not altogether majestic hook off his eyebrows to the square leg boundary. The over ended in uproar with Kite conferring with Filbert and then talking to Hunt who called Fitzgerald over. There were loud shouts that the 'bloody Irishman' should go back home or be placed under lock and key. Again Fitzgerald tapped his forehead in that strange, thoughtful way. There was a suggestion of a shrug as he took his sweater but I could swear he never opened his mouth.

The tea interval was its usual short self. There was just time for Festing to replenish his whisky and to push the pink gin into my protesting hands, while Thirtle consulted an ancient *Wisden* drawn from his capacious canvas bag. Then they were off again with Hindmarsh from the Pavilion End. It was uneventful but the quiet ended when Hunt gave Fitzgerald the ball for the next over. A blast of disapproval swept the ground, the perfect recipe for disturbing a batsman's concentration. But there was no reaction from Fitzgerald. He had two listless overs but in spite of these Byron appeared restless. He flashed twice at Hindmarsh who, sensing his opportunity, bowled him a beauty that nipped in from the off. Byron, caught in two minds, got an inside edge and the ball flew to Roper. It was a difficult chance but the wicket-keeper, diving to his left, got the ball in his glove, and promptly dropped it. It was the first let-off of the day. At the end of the over Hunt had a word with Fitzgerald who, rather out of character, seemed to be nodding in agreement. It seemed likely that he would be taken off. Just one more over perhaps.

He took the ball and walked back very slowly to his mark. His first two deliveries to Kirkstead were sluggish. A single brought Byron to face him. Fitzgerald now looked substantially changed. Suddenly his action disintegrated, the rhythm, control and co-ordination had vanished, his feet dragged and his arm drooped. Three deliveries to Byron were all drained of life and spirit, and the ball almost had a struggle to reach the other end. Byron seemed at once infected by the same disease, pushing feebly forward, as though reluctant to inflict punishment. There was one ball left.

For the first time Fitzgerald pulled his arm across his brow, wiping away a thick film of sweat. He wagged his head like an old dog beaten by the heat of the day. Festing's pipe had gone out and I saw that my glass was empty. Fitzgerald began his run. He was staggering now, swaying perceptibly. I was sure he would never reach the wicket. But he did, just. He stumbled up, falling forward slightly, then with one final effort brought the ball up above his head. Then he crumpled and fell at the feet of the umpire. He lay quite still, clutching the ball in his outstretched hand. At first I thought the ripple of noise was the thunder back again but it was the crowd, recording an ominous murmur of dismay.

For the second time that day a player was carried from the field and again I closed my eyes but this time there was utter darkness and no images on the screen. At my side Festing struck a match and the smell of his exotic tobacco entered my nostrils. I felt intolerably tired. I shivered in the heat, there was ice in my belly and a sense of dread, the onset of the fever of panic. I was appalled by my own weakness. How could I be at the mercy of these groundless fears? And if not groundless, according to the President, what then? I just had to pull myself together, to get the work done, to find out the truth, to settle the matter with Julia, to stop lying, or half-lying, to my wife. I was afraid of myself and must stop it. And when I heard Festing's voice in my ear I opened my eyes and decided to stop it there and then.

'Are you all right?' He sounded just like me talking to Brooke-Stanley.

'Yes, yes. I was just thinking that I didn't like the look of that at all.'

'Let's go and find out,' said Festing, standing up. 'We're both big enough.'

'Thirtle, keep an eye on the game, there's a good chap, we won't be long.'

'It's probably heat-stroke,' said Thirtle, 'or a form of enteritis. There was a similar incident in . . .'

We left him talking to himself and went to the pavilion. Mooles was restored to his post by the door and welcomed us with the aplomb of an undertaker. The talk was pitched rather high but there was no fuss or bother. Hunt was off the field and Kirkstead too, I believed. And Kite was missing. The rest of them out in the middle were talking or sitting on the grass. We went upstairs to try our luck, cautiously, in the Australian dressing room. But there we were checked. I saw Brooke-Stanley, who looked straight through me, and Ralph Stiell, the doctor, brushed me aside. This was no place for us and we went down again. It was a long wait and the crowd grew restless. An announcement was long overdue. When it came we learned nothing of Fitzgerald but that the cricket would start again in ten minutes' time. There was a half-hearted cheer.

'I wish to God it would rain,' said Festing.

'Yes, indeed.'

And really that was the extent of our conversation. I saw Festing shove his pipe into his pocket and thought he might

set fire to himself, not for the first time. I went out front and
looked for Julia but she was not in her seat. I thought of
Polly Parsons' hat with the rose in it, Brooke-Stanley's arti-
ficial smile and the hard-backed chairs in that dusty room.
It seemed, oddly enough, a most appropriate place to wait,
especially as Festing was beginning to eye the crowded bar
behind the Long Room.

'I'm going to the lavatory,' he said. 'Don't go away. We'll
have a drink when I get back.'

But when Festing returned I had gone. At least that's what
he said later and I do recall Francis (the guardian of the
broom cupboard) plucking at my sleeve and telling me that
the President wanted to see me without delay and that this
time he was waiting for me in the Secretary's office. The
'broom cupboard', he said confidentially, was occupied by
the President's special guests. Who could they be, I wondered? The cleaners, perhaps? Well, the President wasn't
waiting for me. When I got there the place was deserted. In
the outer office a girl made a hopeless gesture when I asked
her where everyone was. In Forester's office I sat down in
the uncomfortable chair that faced his empty desk. There
was a light, firm step behind me – a housemaster, an assassin, a woman – so light a foot will ne'er wear out the everlasting flint. But it was Brooke-Stanley, using someone else's
office with a confident air of possession. He sat down at the
desk and said :

'Fitzgerald is dead.'

'Of what?'

'Well, heart failure for one thing.'

'And . . .'

'There's something else . . . there's bound to be.'

'What does Stiell say?'

'He's suspicious – and keeping quiet about it.'

'He's told you.'

'I should think so. Who else?'

'And you're telling me –'

'Because I know you won't go off and write about it. And

34

I've told you something already. Couldn't keep it entirely to myself, you know. I can trust you.'

'Yes, you can,' I said in complete sincerity. 'But whatever you suspect, you may not be alone. I think Festing knows something. What happens now?'

'The game goes on, of course. Now at least we've a chance of winning it.' And he chuckled heartily, a surprisingly unforced reaction.

'And Fitzgerald?'

'He'll be joining Abbott at the hospital – as a dead man of course.'

'Something must be said – and written,' I added, with a shudder at the thought of this interminable day stretching ahead.

'Oh, the death will be confirmed soon enough. You can talk about *that*. It will leak out anyway. For the rest . . .'

'Just what is the rest?' I broke in.

'The rest is murder.'

The President stood up, again with the maddening air of a man detained against his will. 'Come to the house tonight when you're through with your work.'

'Oh sure. Not thinking of going to bed early, are you?'

'Don't lose your cool,' he said, wincing immediately at this unfortunate phrase that suited neither his nature nor the situation. 'Francis will have a cold supper waiting for you. And you really must try the Léoville-Poyferré.'

'I have promised to go to Julia's.'

'Good heavens, you'll find time for that, all right.'

'Perhaps she ought to come along too. Might save endless explanations.'

'Certainly not. Why must explanations be endless anyway?'

And he was gone. Suddenly he seemed very fit and receptive. Disaster appeared to suit him.

The cricket did not restart at the time announced and there was little more than forty minutes' play before the close at 6.30. The crowd was informed that Coonan would take the field as substitute for Fitzgerald, and that was all. Or nearly all. There was still tension, but of a more subdued variety. Eyre came on, bowling medium-pace, straight and without penetration. But batsmen get out to this sort of bowling as they do to any other, and it was Byron on 65 who gave a simple return catch to the bowler and also an unwelcome opportunity for Rippon to join Kirkstead for the last two overs. But, in the prevailing circumstances, with so much damage and disaster already on his mind, even Hunt seemed reluctant to disturb him and the day ended with England at 160 for 5 and Abbott retired hurt.

There was a good story here and I made an effort to write it. It was not until later in the evening that Fitzgerald's death was made official. After collapsing on the field he had been examined by a doctor, rushed to hospital and pronounced dead on arrival. But, as I suspected, rumours of his death were around the ground before the close. Forester sensibly came to the Press box and admitted under pressure that it was feared that Fitzgerald may indeed have died of a heart attack. The office, predictably, sent along a young news reporter called Smith to help and hinder me. The eventual front and back page stories had that unique blend of repetition and contradiction which never fails to confuse the reader. Young Smith's poetry proved to be no better than his cricket and he managed to confuse Byron with Shelley. But after phoning and filing and topping and tailing and swearing not to vanish, or at any rate and at all costs to keep in touch with the Sports Editor, I finished my work about 8.15.

The heat that had persisted all day showed no signs of giving up. Nor did Festing. He had not reproached me for deserting him in the pavilion but sat out the rest of play in another part of the Press box. He was a Sunday paper man and had no work to do this day but he stayed around until I had done, keeping an eye on me, and he emerged from the pavilion in the rear as I passed by on my way out.

'Jack. Come home for a drink, and a bite, perhaps.'

Festing lived nearby in Hamilton Terrace. It was a gesture he had often made before.

'I don't think so, Reg. I've had enough today. Enough cricket, anyway.'

'Oh come on, I've been waiting for you.'

There were still people about and a man came up to me and began asking silly questions. Festing took my arm and steered me away. 'Now one good turn . . .'

'All right. But I have an appointment. Hang on. I'll get the car.' It was not until I reached the car park that I realized the car would not be there. I had quite forgotten I had left it at home. But it was a short walk only. We walked in silence and turned off to Festing's flat in the basement of a house he had owned for years. The slight chill that goes with all basements, however elegant, was refreshing. I sat in Festing's best armchair and reached for the phone beside it.

'Just two or three calls.'

'Be my guest.' He went into the kitchen and started clinking and chinking.

I rang Julia. She answered promptly.

'It's me and I'll be late.'

'Where are you?'

'Close at hand.'

'Take care, then. It's been a bad day for cricketers.'

Then I phoned my wife.

'Peggy,' I said stiffly, 'have you heard the news?'

'Yes. What on earth has been happening?'

'I don't know. I'm trying to find out.'

'That means you won't be home tonight?'

'That's right,' I said unpleasantly.

She put the phone down. I cursed, then rang the office.

'What's the latest?' asked Willie.

'There isn't any latest. By now you probably know more than I do.'

'Now, now. Where are you?'

'Somewhere safe and sound. But I'm moving on. I'll ring you in an hour.'

Festing returned with a long gin drink, not too strong. He took an old pipe from the mantelpiece and began fiddling.

'Who killed Cock Robin?' he asked.

'Cock Robin probably had a weak heart. I can think of at least one bastard who should have dropped dead when bowling to me.'

'He was as strong as a bull.'

'It often takes them that way,' I said flippantly. 'What are you getting at?'

'Hunt won't be sorry. There was nearly a nasty fight at Nottingham.'

'Fitzgerald was always fighting.' But I didn't sound convincing.

There had in fact been a recent scuffle in a Nottingham hotel. Two years back Fitzgerald had had an affair with Hunt's wife. She was a silly woman. Hunt had divorced her and Fitzgerald dropped her. She was now living with a barman in Sydney. My judgement of her softened as I recalled her exquisitely shaped hands, so much at odds with the rest of her body and her coarse, physical disposition.

'I'm no expert,' said Festing, blowing smoke at last, 'but that was some stroke, some heart attack.'

'I should shut up and wait and see.'

'I'm sorry,' Festing said patiently. 'But it seems obvious to me that your reaction to this has been distinctly on the nervous side. I have a feeling that you're holding something back.'

It struck me that Festing was holding back more than I was. But all I said was, 'Now you're a policeman!'

'I was at one time, you know.'

So he was. A young policeman who became a cricket reporter. Shades of John Arlott.

'Then keep up the good work. Thanks for the drink and the use of the phone. I must be going.'

We exchanged kindly smiles.

'It's very intriguing. Look here, if you keep me in your picture, I'll keep you in mine. It's not a bad arrangement.

I'm a better reporter than you are, but then you have the very best connections.'

'In that case,' I said rashly, 'I had better cultivate them rightaway.'

'Of course,' he replied as I went to the door. 'And do give my regards to Brooke-Stanley.'

'Tally ho.'

'And one more thing.' I was now halfway up the steps. 'Do you know Hunt's occupation – other than cricket, that is?'

'It doesn't come to mind.'

'He's a pharmaceutical chemist. Good night, Jack.'

Brooke-Stanley's front door was open (an invariable custom of his in fine weather and when expecting company) and a soft light shone out into the dusk. At the end of the hall Francis had just emerged from a door at the end of the hall. This led to the cellar. Francis had a bottle in each hand.

'Good evening, sir. The President is expecting you.'

This was certainly in the grand manner but then Francis was one of a dying breed, the old retainer who has served the family all his life. And he owed his little job at Lord's to Brooke-Stanley. It was an ideal arrangement for both of them and much resented by Mooles.

The small dining room was lined with dark green paper with a touch of gold. Brooke-Stanley at the head of the table was eating his dinner. I had washed in the upstairs cloakroom but still felt hot and dishevelled beside this elegant old gentleman looking so fresh and relaxed in his white silk dressing gown. The meal was simple and good, the claret excellent. Francis opened a second bottle because the old man had made a big impression on the first one. All that he said of importance was contained in one long speech that seemed rehearsed, so precisely was it delivered, complete with slight hesitations, pregnant pauses and careful stresses.

'It won't surprise you, I'm sure, to learn that Ralph Stiell followed – if you follow *me* – Fitzgerald to the hospital down the road. Stiell is very well known there, he does business with them. He was there for some time and I have since spoken to him. I cannot, will not, perhaps *better* not, go into the details, but there is reason to believe that Fitzgerald's death followed the administration of some powerful drug, stimulant or poison that took some time to act. Meanwhile we must get on with the game. At least cricket will survive. I don't know about the murderer. They do say that one murder leads to another. I've often heard that and I'm sure it must be true. Now it was a very curious thing at Nottingham, you know. I'll tell you about it. This is what Fitzgerald told me, on the Friday at Nottingham. There was an envelope for him at the reception desk of his hotel. It was a cheap, brown envelope with his name typed on it. Nothing more, no stamp even. And inside there was a picture postcard of the castle – one of those coloured shiny things. And on the back there was a typewritten message. "Withdraw from the Lord's Test or it will be the final one for you." That's all, nothing more.

'Fitzgerald did nothing about this. You know that he was an odd, secretive man as well as a violent one. I'm not sure if you knew how morbid, superstitious, even *frightened* he could be. He was afraid of horses, thunderstorms, the dark – you know the sort of thing. But again, when he was a lad he rushed into a blazing house to rescue a child. He was badly burned but he brought out the child. It was dead . . . As for Nottingham, I tend to believe that he was fit all right and that he was left out because of other factors. It could have been the selectors who were worried about his character – shall we say? Or it could have been Fitzgerald protesting that he was simply unwell and even unwilling. But this is guesswork on my part. He got a second postcard on the Sunday, at the same place and in a similar envelope. There was an identical picture of the castle and another typed message. This one said (it was rather comical in fact): "If you play at Lord's you will wake up dead." . . . Now he never *showed* me these cards or the envelopes. I have no evidence at all that they ever existed and I never thought to ask him if he inquired as to how they got there or who delivered them. Perhaps if they turn up I shall have to go to the police. Perhaps I ought to go right away, but I don't know, I'm sure. Indeed, I should have told *him* to go to the police because I had a strong feeling myself that his life was in danger. But I didn't, you know. I felt sorry for him, this rather unpleasant man who took me into his confidence after a drink or two, but I didn't care for him at all. I don't entirely share the view of cricket writers like that fanatic, Festing, that the "new" fast bowling is more deadly and intimidating than that of the past. But he's nearer the mark than I'd care to admit. But today when Fitzgerald was bowling . . . there was something unbalanced about it all. I'm sure he was afraid for his life. Perhaps he'd had a hint, another ridiculous note. It sounds a ludicrous tale but I haven't told a soul apart from you.'

Brooke-Stanley stopped talking and sipped his port, without relish it appeared. He looked exhausted and I, too, was feeling the fatigue that must have shown in my face.

I stood up. 'It's bedtime, Philip. We'll talk tomorrow.'

He nodded. 'But what do you think, Jack?'

He sounded rather plaintive now, but I was of no help.

'I don't know what to think.'

There was a gold clock in the dining room. It stood in a corner where there was plenty of room for expression. It had a thin, piercing chime and had the same effect on conversation as if a bomb had dropped. I hadn't noticed it before that evening but now I was aware it was chiming midnight and that the first, long day of the Test Match had ended.

Then Brooke-Stanley joined in on the final stroke.

'By the way, you remember Francis Thompson, the only man who has written a really good poem about cricket?'

'Yes. Hornby and Barlow. "And the run stealers flicker to and fro".'

'That's the man.'

'What about him?'

'He died in 1907 – in the hospital down the road.'

Friday

Julia's flat was big and comfortable and at the top of the block. In a high wind the doors rattled but the lifts were always working, the porters on duty and the shopkeepers still delivered the goods. I had seen the lights from the road and I knew she was still up: I had a key but I rang the bell. She opened the door and said, 'Haven't you got a key?'

'Well yes, but . . . oh never mind.'

I went into the sitting room that was as long as a cricket pitch and as high as a church steeple. The lights were dim. Polly Parsons lay on a sofa, drinking something. She was wearing the one pair of pyjamas I kept at Julia's place and she went into them very well. Julia was wearing a long dress, or nightgown, that revealed nothing.

'Jack, you look terrible,' said Julia. The smile on her face seemed stronger than the concern in her voice.

I sprawled in a big chair at the far end of the room, away from Polly.

'I would like some lemon juice with ice and water.'

'We have just that. Polly, earn your keep.'

Polly swung off the sofa and undulated out of the room.

'Hope you don't mind about the pyjamas. Polly's staying the night and she grabbed them from the bedroom.'

'I don't mind at all,' I said, peering through the smoke haze and coughing slightly. The smell of rich tobacco and expensive scent lingered in the heat. 'Yes, I'm tired. I've been having dinner with Philip.'

'I thought as much.'

She looked fresh but rather frantic. Then Polly returned

with the lemon juice. She looked tired, even worried, but her face scrubbed clean of make-up shone with astonishing health. 'There you are. Now I'm off to bed.'

'Good night, then,' said Julia. 'Don't forget, bright and early. I have a hairdo at nine sharp and Mrs Gates is due at nine fifteen.'

Polly smiled, blew a kiss and left.

'I want to go to bed too,' I said.

'So you shall, darling.'

The lemon juice was cold and astringent. Julia sat down and maddeningly lit another cigarette. I could now see the outline of her long legs under the stuff she was wearing. A small flame broke from the embers of desire. Her lips opened slightly and I saw the tip of her tongue sliding between her teeth but her eyes were still and watchful, though there was still the hint of a smile. A wave of bad temper swept my desire away.

'You'll smoke yourself to death,' I said weakly.

She looked at her watch. 'Willie rang just after midnight. He'll still be there.'

I had forgotten my promise to Willie. I went to the phone and got him immediately. What I knew or suspected, I couldn't tell him. There were no reproaches, no heavy humour; Willie, though persistent, had a delicate touch. He seemed to detect at once my fatigue and frustration and he cut the conversation short. We agreed to talk in the morning. Then Julia, too, seemed to abandon inclination to talk and inquire. She stood up and said, 'There's a robe in the bathroom. I'll see you shortly.'

I had a shower, a rather long and cold one. I went into the bedroom and dropped the bathrobe at the foot of the bed. The clothes were thrown back. Julia was very still. I lay on my side and looked at her. The dark green eyes were wide open and unblinking and shining like a cat's in the dark.

She tugged at the bracelet of my watch.

'It's silly to just keep that on.'

'It's a habit, you know,' I said wearily.

Lightly she pulled the watch from my wrist and placed it behind me on a table by the bed. Then, nude and alert, she came close and began to stroke the inside of my arm. I yawned and she pushed a leg between mine.

'Fitzgerald won't be getting any more of this,' I said. It was a spiteful remark and I was surprised to hear it coming from my mouth.

She came closer still. The hand moved lightly between my elbow and the hollow under my arm. Her sharp nails delicately scored the surface of my skin. The other hand rested flat on my heart.

'Bump, bump, bump,' she whispered, and gently inserted the tip of her tongue into my ear.

The other hand moved to another place.

There was always a special stealth about Julia's approach to love and intercourse. It was so quiet and yet so ominous; the art she practised so skilfully and smoothly was emphasized here and there by some new yet controlled excitement, like a studied irregularity of form. It was an approach that captivated me and filled me with childish fears, like being afraid of the growing darkness, afraid of death. When she really cornered me I was full of dread, and she had me cornered now. Just for a second I realized that this was the time to ask some questions. We were both vulnerable and I might catch her out before the lovemaking began. But she was too quick. The hand on my heart moved swiftly to my belly, pressed it a little, then went down to my roots. Her tongue thrust deeper into my ear. 'There now, we'll soon have you fit again,' she whispered. I tried to get away but she had a very firm grip on me.

'You're hurting me.'

'Not for long, darling. You won't notice it presently.'

With a violent movement I went, amiably enough, for her throat, but found my hands on her breasts. They were small and hard with very big nipples. It was my turn now and I squeezed hard. It was useless. Her moan of ecstasy forced my eyes open and in a flash her tongue came down, pushing between my lips and licking my teeth. I squeezed harder and she released her grip. But the damage was done.

'That's better,' she said, her voice rising and losing a little control.

'Come inside.'

All Julia's movements were quick and supple. In a second she was on top and had me inside her and with her nails, now like claws, at work. But the animal was not entirely out of control. Her rhythm was perfect and I sensed that she was determined to call the tune and, I realized, to take her time and wear me out in the process. But now I was fully roused and in pretty good shape. As her teeth clashed with mine I got the signal from her body that absolute perfection and total ecstasy were still a little way off. With a supreme effort I tried to frustrate this design and beat *her* to it, but she was an expert and we both came together.

I had always thought that her final cry resembled nothing so much as a call for help. And there it was again, piercing the thick night air. Then silence. Julia never uttered a word (to me at any rate) after making love. She put her arms around me, just like a child, seemed to sigh more in triumph than satisfaction and with a typical show of strength gripped me like a vice.

When I woke up the vice was gone. I was aware of the open windows and the curtains standing still in the thick heat. The bedroom door was open and there was a dim light from the hall. Julia was gone but I could smell her scent on my body and on the bed. From the hall, or beyond it, I heard a footfall, a faint cry, then the noise of a car sweeping by below. Totally alert, for I am not one of those who climb reluctantly out of sleep, I got out of bed, put on the robe and checked my watch. It was 4.00 a.m. The hall was deserted. I went on and passed through the open door of the sitting room. It was dark in there, just a faint light from the windows and a faint smell of Black Russians. Julia came from behind the door, one hand resting modestly on the red triangle of her pubic hairs and the other outstretched as if warding something off. Her eyes were half-closed and shining so brightly through the slits that I was glad not to get the full shock of them. She was muttering but I couldn't hear the words, she was sleep-walking and I stood aside to get out of her way. I followed her and she paused by the door where Polly was sleeping. Then she placed both arms behind her head and I became aware of unforeseen, unknown erotic consequences. Her buttocks trembled and she went on and into her own room. She lay on the sheets, shivering and still talking to herself. I tried gently to cover her up and she opened her eyes, staring at me out of the sleep, and cried out in a harsh voice, 'Hurt me, you bastard, hurt me like the time you did on the beach.'

Then, as if released from a spell, she appeared to fall into deep, natural sleep. I listened and waited for a long time but eventually I dropped off too. There must have been many men who had been on a beach with Julia. But I hadn't.

Breakfast was a fully dressed, agreeable affair. We were all up in time and treating one another in that polite, condescending manner that is so characteristic of a well-behaved family. Polly looked fresh in yesterday's clothes and I eyed her with appreciation and curiosity.

'Julia,' she said, 'may I leave my hotel and stay here until the game is over?'

Julia gave her a hard look. 'Yes, you can stay here if you like. You can help with the party tomorrow. But don't give up your hotel room. You may find that it will come in useful. In any event don't bring any of your friends back here, either by day or by night. Understood?'

Polly appeared to consider these blunt conditions and a flash of petulance crossed her large, innocent-looking eyes. Then she said, 'Yes, Julia. Anything you say. What shall I do with Jack's pyjamas?'

'Wash them, you idiot. And you can do some shopping for me at Selfridges.'

I walked to the window and looked at the sky. As ever it was dark and thundery.

'It might rain today,' I said.

'I doubt it,' said Julia, her eyes following Polly who was now reading a newspaper – the one I worked for. 'Are you reading Jack's copy, Polly?'

'No,' she said sweetly, without looking up. 'I can never understand these cricket reports. It says on the front page that Fitzgerald's death is very mysterious.'

'Most deaths are,' said Julia crossly. 'Excuse me. May I?' And she took away the paper from Polly. Then after a moment she said, 'I see there's no mention of you, Polly. All in good time, perhaps.' And she let fly with one of her strange mirthless laughs.

Polly looked at me and blushed, a little mechanically, I thought.

'What was that?' I asked quietly – too quietly, perhaps. Polly said nothing and Julia had turned to the sports pages, in search of me, perhaps. She snorted. ' "The Over of Death". What a headline, and what a terrible picture of Fitzgerald. It must be at least five years old and he looks dead already.'

Julia thrust the paper at me as if she had decided it was my turn to read. I ran through my copy (by no means the first thing I usually did at breakfast). It had been cut but not rewritten and the jumpiness I'd felt when writing it came clearly across.

Then, with astonishment, I heard Julia speaking to Polly and making no effort to keep her voice down. 'Did you give anything to Fitzgerald, by the way, or write a note, or anything of that kind?'

'No,' muttered Polly. 'I didn't. Not at all.'

I lowered the paper. The women were staring at one another.

'I suppose they might find out about ... er ... Nottingham,' said Polly.

Julia laughed again. 'What of it? Don't be stupid. Just let

it be a warning to you not to sleep with strange men.'

Julia smiled at me sympathetically. 'Dear Jack, how little you know. Now I must go and get my hair done. Polly, you may as well leave with me.'

That was to be expected perhaps, but a nuisance all the same. I had hoped for a discreet word with Polly. But obviously, Julia, in spite of her brief outburst – surely intended to be heard by me – had decided I knew enough to be going on with.

'I do hope,' said Julia, straightening my tie, 'that you will be spending the weekend here, Jack. We girls get a little nervous, you know.'

'At night, you mean?'

Was there the slightest reaction in those dark green eyes? I couldn't be sure. There was no reply to my question and I said, 'I'll see, I'll see. I'm not sure about the weekend. But lunch, come what may. I'll see you behind the pavilion.'

Julia nodded briskly. 'Mrs Gates will be here soon. There are no messages. I will be back in an hour or so and I'll talk to her myself. If a whole lot of booze arrives, ask them to dump it in the little room next to mine. And while you're here *do* please answer the phone.'

They left and I went to Julia's huge fridge and rummaged out a quarter bottle of champagne. I poured the wine into a most inappropriate glass and, sitting in a chair by the window, I awaited the arrival of Mrs Gates and contemplated the infinite, or some such foolish thing.

Then the phone started ringing.

The first call, unexpected as it was, freed me for action. It was my wife.

'Peggy,' I said, trying not to sound reproachful, 'you never ring me at this number.'

'Jack,' she replied, seeming to sound understanding, 'I just want to work out the weekend. Are you free to talk?'

'I am alone,' I said as Mrs Gates came through the door. We exchanged comical faces and she retired.

'I'm sorry about Fitzgerald, Jack.'

'Yes, isn't it awful,' I said with a flood of relief, and then with total recklessness, 'He was probably murdered, the bastard.'

'That's shocking,' said Peggy, in the even tone of voice that recalled the very firm set of her mouth. 'But surely you can tell me more than that?'

'No, I can't. Not now.'

'Are you coming home tonight?'

'I don't know.'

'Don't bother,' she said kindly. 'Hester is coming over and ... and I thought you might feel better staying away until it's over.'

'The game, you mean?'

'Well, yes if you like.'

'I see,' I said pointlessly, thinking of something else.

'What you might, ought to do, I think, is come to Sunday lunch with the children and Hester.'

That seemed reasonable enough. Hester was a school friend of Peggy's. And without venom where I was concerned.

'I'll do that.'

'Do you need the car?'

'No.'

'I'll leave a case with some things for you with Mr Corker at the gate.'

'That's not necessary.'

'It probably is,' she replied, betraying for the first time a trace of impatience. 'And,' she added brightly, 'I need a new coat. Nothing special. Just something I have my eye on. Would you leave a cheque for £100 with Mr Corker – sort of fair exchange, no robbery.'

'Yes, darling.'

'Yes, Peggy, you should have said. Try not to be late for lunch.' She rang off. I had known brighter conversations with my wife. These days more bitterness than cheerfulness kept breaking in but her new, sharp, slightly calculating attitude was still not totally devoid of affection.

Mrs Gates came back again. She was a most energetic, desirable woman in her late forties. She was a widow, emphatically not hard done by, utterly without woe or self-pity and a born organizer. There was a certain resemblance to Julia. She had the same infuriating grace of looking attractive in the most unlikely positions. She opened her mouth to speak as the door bell rang, and after that the phone. I took the phone off the cradle but spoke to Mrs Gates.

'Good morning, Eileen. If that's the men with the drink tell them to dump it down the hall . . .'

I spoke to the phone. It was my Sports Editor, curt but courteous.

'Jack, when may I see you?'

'Right away, Willie. Come round to Abbey Road.'

I went to the door. It was indeed the drink, carried in with sullen dedication by those who would like a quick one themselves. Mrs Gates saw them in and out, then disappeared to return in a smart red nylon dust coat that buttoned up the front.

'Julia's at the hairdresser,' I said. 'She'll be back. Would you please leave the sitting room till last.'

'Right. Coffee?'

'When my friend arrives. It'll be Mr Williamson.'

I returned to my champagne and tried to compose my feelings for the day's events. There was the game, the 'pure cricket' as I liked to call it. There was a job to be done there and it must be the main one. In the Fitzgerald business, some things would be made clear, others probably not. Brooke-Stanley and Festing could not be avoided and I might pursue some small investigations of my own. Proceed cautiously, but involvement now seemed inevitable. The trouble was that I might find out too much. Both Julia and Polly knew more – if only a little more – than they pretended. But was there in fact any pretence? Only reluctance maybe. Don't exaggerate, don't jump to conclusions. Then there was Dr Stiell. He was certainly more of an acquaintance than a friend and anyway he might just clam up professionally. Could I 'get at him' where others might not? It was worth a try. But avoid muddle. Concentrate, concentrate. Treat each ball on its merits and stop thinking about the next one. Build and construct the innings with care, but punish the loose stuff at all times. 'There is probably' (I quote the great Bradman again) 'a greater premium on temperament for a batsman than for any player in any branch of sport.' Well, I had been a batsman. I had tried to play the unplayable, stayed at the crease just long enough to lick my lips, and stayed and dominated for two days without giving a chance. I had mostly got out doing one thing while thinking of another. Yet some risks would have to be taken in the course of the present enterprise. Physical stamina and mental stamina and a sustained state of exceptional alertness would be required. I finished the champagne. I took the glass and bottle to the kitchen. And on my way back through the hall I wondered why Julia had walked in the night.

The phone again. It was Brooke-Stanley.

'Just to inform you,' said the President in a powerful voice that was the reverse of confidential, 'that the post-mortem will be conducted later today by Hawthorne.'

'Very well.' Sir Nigel Hawthorne was a leading Home Office pathologist.

'He is an old friend of the Stiell family. Detests cricket, but oddly enough saw the incident on television. I've read your cricket report. Rather emotional, I thought,' added this brusque, yet deeply emotional old man.

'I'll apply more reason next time.'

'Yes, we could do with some of that. I'll be in touch.'

The buzzing and whining of Mrs Gates's hoovering in other rooms and in the hall first irritated and then relaxed me. I became somnolent and dozy. Then the door bell sounded a different note. Willie came in with shadows under his eyes. I looked at him too long.

'I see you're looking at the shadows under my eyes,' he said.

'That's right. Sit down. Mrs Gates will bring some coffee.'

'The Editor,' said Willie, 'sees a big story on our hands, but in his infinite wisdom has asked me to deal directly with you in regard to both cricket and the, er, complications.'

'I don't know much about the complications, as you call them.'

'Don't you? We believe that Hawthorne has a special job in hand. Surely you know about that?'

'I cannot tell a lie,' I said fatuously, feeling again that intense annoyance when one's confidential information is in everyone else's possession. 'I was given the same information just before you arrived.'

'So?'

'As you assume, there's a possibility that Fitzgerald was murdered.'

'And?'

'I can't say more than that, Willie.'

'Other people might.'

'Then they would be foolish to say so, at this stage. I will do my best for you, for the paper, for your public and for my conscience.'

'I should hope so,' Willie smiled bleakly. We drank coffee in silence. Then he said, 'I won't push you any more at the present. Now there's a fair amount of space for tomorrow. Could you find time to do an appreciation of Fitzgerald – say 600 words?'

'Yes.'

He took some cuttings from his pocket. 'All the background's here, age, education, first games of any consequence, etc. That should save you some trouble.'

'Good.' I took the cuttings and stuffed them in my pocket. 'I'll put it over after lunch.'

'Smith will be along again. Do you mind?'

'No, not really,' I said honestly. 'I hope he's done his homework this time.'

'Yes, he has.'

The conversation drifted until Julia came in. I glanced at

my watch. She had been away for eighty minutes. Time was in a hurry today.

'Don't get up. Hello Willie. Plotting?'

'Just a few quick singles,' I said.

'Of course. Would you like some more champagne, Jack?'

'Ah, you've been in the kitchen.' I gave her a hard look.

'No, thank you. Have some coffee?'

'Eileen's seeing to it.'

'That was pretty quick for you.' I eyed Julia's hair. 'It looks just the same to me.'

She smiled sweetly and handed me a parcel. 'It's about time you had a new shirt. I got this at the little shop that's closing down.'

It was a fine shirt with blue and white vertical stripes.

'Why, thank you, Julia.'

Willie, politely, began to read a rival newspaper. The odd groan escaped him.

'Any calls?' Julia asked as the phone began again.

'It's never stopped. And all for me.'

She answered and said, 'Hello. Yes he is. Indeed. See you tomorrow. Any old time after eight. You can help Jack with the drinks.' She handed me the phone.

'You've been much engaged,' said Reg Festing. His voice sounded thick.

'I'm much in demand today.'

'Not a bad piece, Jack. A bit cryptic perhaps.'

'Not too emotional?' I inquired skittishly.

'Ah, there's no hope for you there. You should have stayed in the game longer, you know. You'll never be knighted now.'

'Reg,' I said plainly and politely, 'what can I do for you?'

'Quite a bit, I should imagine. To begin with, you'll be going to the cricket?'

'Of course. Aren't you?'

'Keep an eye on things. I have a few calls to make. I'll be along in the afternoon.'

'Good. You wouldn't like me to write your Sunday piece, by any chance?'

'What's that?'

'You heard. God is not mocked, especially where Australian fast bowlers are concerned.'

'Good-bye for now, my friend.' And with his well-known impersonation of a dead Press Lord, he rang off.

Julia was sitting on the sofa with Mrs Gates. They also appeared to be putting on an act – the mother and daughter act – one of those relationships that suggest intimacy by way of aloofness. I yawned and refused to break a silence that was verging on the border of sullenness. Then Willie stood up to go. He bowed to Julia and Mrs Gates and said to me, 'Right then, skipper. Let's see how it goes. I don't think I'll make the cricket today.'

'Not to worry. I will be here tonight. If I'm a little late my secretary – that's the one with red hair – will take a message.'

Willie left and Mrs Gates stood up and surveyed Julia's beautiful carpet.

'You know, *Miss*, you really should have a drugget to put down. They'll make an awful mess – all those cricketers and journalists.'

'But you will be here to restrain them, Eileen,' said Julia with a sudden crossing and uncrossing of her legs aimed in my direction.

Mrs Gates removed cups and saucers to the kitchen. Julia had a coughing bout then rummaged in her bag to produce the black cigarette pack and the silver lighter.

'Are you staying on, then?' she asked.

'Yes. I'll be here throughout the weekend.'

'That's very nice.'

'I must go home to lunch on Sunday.'

'Good.'

The phone rang again and she answered it.

'It's for me this time,' she said.

'I'm off to the ground.'

'Don't go on my account.'

But her hand was tightly over the mouthpiece. I felt a sudden thump of jealousy. She wanted me, just now, out of the way. I was certain of it. With a simple physical gesture and a few words she had roused again, infallibly, my desires and emotions and made me very angry. I picked up the shirt, threw it down childishly and left.

Arriving at Lord's I spotted Merryweather by the pavilion. The head groundsman was the perfection of his type; strong, square, tanned, hardworking and friendly. He came from Gloucestershire and was apt to mutter 'Wally Hammond' from time to time. Years ago, as a boy and dogsbody he had known Hedley Verity and Jack Hobbs. Occasionally they got into his conversation too.

'Well, sir?' He looked at me, then at the sky.

'Well, what indeed. How about the weather?'

'Like yesterday. Very hot and no rain but a bit darker — until lunchtime at any rate.'

'And the wicket?' I asked cautiously.

'It will play for a fortnight, sir. Full of runs.'

'I'm glad to hear it.'

'Now that Mr Fitzgerald's *gone*,' he added awkwardly, 'there won't be that roughing up. It's a shame to ruin a wicket in that fashion.'

'Yes, I suppose Herbie Kite is not actually crying his eyes out?'

'No, sir,' said Merryweather cautiously. 'You know umpires.'

'Indeed I do. They are all for a quiet life. They have my sympathy. I would rather be a groundsman myself.'

Merryweather smiled politely and left. I turned to confront Mooles who had clearly been listening to our conversation. He smiled unpleasantly.

'A game to remember, I'd say, Mr Stenton.'

'This is not the sinking of the *Titanic*, Mooles,' I said severely as I caught Corker's eye on his way to the Grace Gates.

'Mr Corker, a word.'

'Certainly, sir.'

I went to Corker's little office by the gate, gave him the cheque for Peggy and asked him to look after the suitcase she was bringing me. Corker was a splendid, imperturbable character. In his ideal world cricket would have existed not only without spectators, but without cricketers as well. 'They get in the way, sir,' he would say, shaking his head like a man contemplating a vast army in defence of its homeland, 'they get in the way.'

To prove his point a man stopped, thrust his scorecard at me and asked for my autograph. I signed it and he looked astonished.

'What's the matter?'

'I'm sorry,' and he backed away in confusion. 'Thank you very much but I thought you were someone else.'

'You see what I mean, sir,' said Corker with a sadistic, triumphant gleam in his eye.

'Indeed I do, Corker. Now Francis Thompson would never have made that mistake.'

'Thompson, Francis Thompson? Didn't he play for Sussex, sir, or was it Lancashire?'

Merryweather was right about the weather. It was hot, humid and dark, but just light enough to play cricket. We all learned (including the crowd) that though Abbott hoped to take a further part in the game, he would not bat again in this innings, nor would he be available in the field when Australia's turn came to bat. And so England were effectively 160 for 6, with Kirkstead and Rippon to resume, and the bowlers Ackroyd, Mappleton and Standish to come. There is an old saying that 'now the stars are out, the batsmen can start making runs'. But not every 'tail' furiously wags the dog. And in England's case today, I thought it doubtful.

Hindmarsh and Eyre opened the Australian attack. Kirkstead, that valiant man in a crisis, soon found the present situation too much for his technical resources. Eyre, the medium-pacer moving the ball both ways with or without intent, looked at once most difficult to cope with. He had a spell typical of Bill Johnston or Alec Bedser in their heyday. Kirkstead knew all about this kind of bowling, indeed he excelled in it himself, but the batting is another matter. He was out driving Eyre to a ball that left him at the last, tantalizing moment. He got an edge and Madden with consummate ease took a sharp chance on the slips. Ackroyd came in and looked awful but he surprisingly edged and flashed his way to 18 before Hindmarsh laid the wicket flat with a dead-straight delivery of perfect length and exceptional velocity. As soon as Mappleton came in, Rippon was out lbw to Eyre. Standish, renowned as one of the world's worst batsmen, came in for the bitter end. We were then treated to one of those last-wicket stands that crop up so frequently in the first-class game when bowlers who supposedly cannot bat, score quite a few useful runs. Standish, a fine, accurate fast bowler in the Statham mould, but with batting feet of lead, kept hitting the ball with the middle of a worn, yellow bat and scored five boundaries. Then Hunt, more shrewd than exasperated, I suspected, brought on Flinders and he promptly bowled Standish with a leg break that would have crawled round a brick wall. It was 12.45. England were 223 for 9, with Abbott retired hurt. The innings was over.

I stayed in the Press box, writing my Fitzgerald piece. I was, and looked, I'm sure, in a bearish mood and found it necessary to growl only at Thirtle who started muttering about O'Reilly. Then just on one o'clock Hunt and Burnett came out to open the Australian innings. During this brief intermission the light had improved immensely and the ground was now packed solid. Lincoln, the young Derbyshire all-rounder, took the field in place of Abbott, and Mappleton and Standish opened the attack. Hunt, lithe and quick-footed, was one of the more engaging opening batsmen of the world scene. His partner, Burnett, was a tall, muscular man who never seemed to open his broad shoulders. His stroke play was limited but stylish and he was very difficult to shift unless he was nailed early on. At lunch, after thirty minutes, this pair had put on 35 with very little trouble. Kirkstead, as acting captain, had put Lincoln into the covers in place of Abbott. This proved costly against Hunt's driving. The twelfth man was an extremely fit, young and keen county cricketer. Promising perhaps, but posted on the field in these circumstances he showed traces of nerves. His anticipation was at fault and he tended to move the wrong way. Later, in another position, he settled down.

I had lunch as arranged with Julia, eating little and drinking nothing. I was struck again by her sure instinct for the precise nature of another person's mood. Not that mine was all that difficult to detect. I was cross and sullen and not in the mood for conversation. She who had always known how to get at me was equally confident in the matter of leaving me alone. She chatted quietly about the cricket and predicted that in spite of the now all-too-permanent absence of Fitzgerald (a superb middle-order batsman had been another of his attributes), Australia would make a big score with a substantial lead in the first innings. I grunted my agreement and then, in a fit of sociability, asked her where Polly was. She had no idea and then managed a touch of concern when she went on to ask me if I minded sleeping with her while Polly was under the same roof? That didn't bother me at all, I replied. Yet it did somehow. Then would I be back for dinner, say between eight and nine? That I couldn't tell. Not to worry. She would be going home as soon as the game was over. There was a lot to do, preparing for the party on Saturday. But if I wanted her to meet me somewhere for a drink, why then she'd be delighted, she'd meet me anywhere within reason – or even without it, she added gently. There was always time for the more important things of life. She gave me a sharp and friendly kick on the shin and almost restored my good humour.

After lunch and back in the Press box – curiously deserted, it seemed to me – I finished my piece on Fitzgerald and put it over to the office. It fell a bit short, both in length and performance, I thought – but I had little stomach for it. I had thought in the morning, before I began to write, that I might infuse it with a little spirit, spite or even a fair degree of objective judgement. But it all turned sour in the execution – you might say – and I was left with the conviction that I had let the dead man down. I knew now that he had slept with Polly, and had a brooding suspicion he had done the same with Julia. But now that he was over and done with, surely he could be left alone for ever? Perhaps it would take a little time, at least the length of a five-day Test Match. I turned back to the cricket.

At tea Australia were 125 for 2. Considering there were no wickets down at four o'clock there was a hint of brightness in England's outlook. Both the openers had reached their fifties before Ackroyd – a bowler much in the manner and style of Underwood – bowled, quite without warning, both of them in one over. Maitland and Madden, the first two of the trio from New South Wales, then played comfortably until tea. Perhaps my thoughts were very much elsewhere but it is a stage of the game that I can scarcely remember.

At tea I had tea, for a change. There was no word from Brooke-Stanley and no sign of Reg Festing. The weather was still uncomfortable and rather hard on the nerves. Odd rumbles of thunder, as on Thursday, but still no sign of rain for refreshment, and still the same infuriating condition of light that by now both players and spectators had become accustomed to. In the Press box, even Thirtle seemed subdued and Ransley, I noticed, had nodded off. After tea I went for a walk round the ground. The bars were doing well and the betting tent booming. But I was not in the betting mood. I met two former Test players, one cheerful and drunk, the other as boring and sober as I was. The game sounded very quiet indeed. Back at the Press box the steward at the foot of the stairs handed me a note. It was from Brooke-Stanley.

Francis stood aside to admit me to the room in the rear of the pavilion. The President was alone and drinking. 'First today,' he said encouragingly. 'Dammit, I'll have my second.' In a fit of inspired weakness I seized a bottle and poured myself a hefty gin. Then we both sat down.

'Good cricket?' he asked.

'I don't know. I don't think so, but then I haven't quite got into it today,' I replied.

'Madden's a great player,' he said absently. 'He just seems to pick his spot – and hits it there.'

'Hum.' My mood was still fragile and I was in no state for the President's oblique approach.

'There were delays,' he said, 'but the foul play I suspected is now more or less confirmed. Yesterday, almost certainly in the tea interval, Fitzgerald took something that killed him. He imbibed a powerful drug, virtually tasteless in tea, lemonade, beer ... those sort of things. It might not have killed him had he kept still after taking it, but the violent exercise of, say, fast bowling, made it virtually inevitable.'

'Could he have ministered it himself?'

'Certainly. But why should he do that?'

'Is it totally ruled out?' I persisted.

'Not entirely, I suppose,' he said with his sudden, frosty smile. 'But what do you think?'

'I think he was murdered.'

And I poured both of us some more gin.

'Who knows about this?'

'Soon everyone will. But it will be the "foul play is suspected" sort of thing. There'll be a lot of fuss and muddle until it's cleared up. If it ever is.'

The President looked dejected. I was puzzled. 'Have you lost interest, then?' I inquired.

'By no means. There might be another one.'

'Another one?'

'Another murder, of course. You see, if we try hard enough we shall probably find out who it is.'

'We? Do you mean you and me?'

'Yes. And Festing perhaps. He's nosing around, as you thought.'

'Who else?'

He shrugged. 'Oh, there may be one or two others. Then there's the police, of course. There's a man called Green. Very sharp, very good at his cricket. Used to play for a Middlesex Sunday league side.'

I groaned.

'You'll like him,' said the President. 'By the way, he knows Festing. But he's a bit wary of him.'

There was a roar from the crowd outside.

'I must try to concentrate and write,' I said. 'I must go back.'

'But of course. Are you looking in tonight?'

'I might. I'll ring.'

'You're very welcome. We must meet again soon, you know. There are still matters, quite crucial matters, that we haven't discussed. I'm relying on your help and your confidence.'

Something about his attitude provoked me to sudden warmth. I clutched his shoulder. 'Don't worry, Philip. In spite of the experts I am sure we are due for some rain. It could put an end to all our problems.'

'Then let it come down,' he said.

I left the President's office to find Festing looking at me over his shoulder. 'Maitland's out,' he said, 'off Mappleton in the slips. Easy one.'

'There are no easy ones in the slips,' I said shortly, and turned away.

Festing followed me to the Press box and sat nearby and in silence until the end of the game. I learned that Smith had been looking for me and would be back. More groaning and gritting, then for the first time that day I plunged head-long into the cricket. It could have been worse. Musgrave had joined Madden and these two aggressive batsmen cut loose and by the close Australia were 255 for 3. The England attack, though tired, never quite went to pieces and the fielding stayed admirably sharp with young Lincoln running his feet off at third man. Smith turned up again but I shrugged him off obstinately until 7.30 when I reckoned I'd done a sound and responsible job, though with a touch of the hum-drums.

Festing loomed. 'Reg,' I said sharply. 'I want a few minutes with Mr Smith. I'll see you at the Rossetti, not a minute later than 8.30.'

'Why not at my place?'

'Because I prefer the pub. See you.'

Smith was tired. The findings of the inquest had not been published, of course, and all that was known was that it was not a straightforward case of sudden heart failure and that further tests, analyses and investigations would have to be made. Smith was not a crime reporter and was relieved to have just learned from the office that one of the paper's heavy mob would be following up the case and that he had to brief him and that there was an urgent need for me to come too. I turned that down flat by saying that although I had no exclusive information I was doing my best to acquire some and that I must do it in my own way and that further-more the Sports Editor knew this and the Editor had been or should have been informed accordingly. If the paper had not heard from me by ten o'clock they could reach me without fail at a certain number (already in their posses-sion). I was sorry but I knew nothing for certain, nothing worth saying. I had already pronounced on Fitzgerald the cricketer and I had neither the skills nor the sources to pro-vide them with – at best – some very dubious assumptions. I would do what I could and ring as soon as possible.

'I'm sorry, Mr Smith, this may sound confused, even a little contradictory but that's all I can say just now. Tell them to count on nothing. Who knows, you might find out something for yourself. Try the phone book for a start.'

I ended rather more sharply than I had begun, but I was getting tense again and didn't need Smith to depress me when I could do that job much more efficiently myself. I left him and walked to meet Festing. I was there a little early but he called to me outside the pub where he was sitting at one of the small tables under the branches of one huge tree. He'd kept a seat for me and a drink ready, the trusting soul. He grinned. 'You are beginning to resemble nothing so much as a harassed, ageing journalist.'

'It's Saturday tomorrow, thank God. Then *you* can sweat a bit,' I said cheerfully.

'You'll have all day to find things out. Then we can compare notes at Julia's party.'

'I shall drink and tell lies,' I answered.

He sipped a most powerful-looking scotch and I looked suspiciously at my gin.

'They're a bit on the strong side, but it's getting very crowded in there and I can see you're in no mood for hanging around.'

'That's right. Now then.'

'Well now you *know* what we both suspected. Fitzgerald was murdered.'

'It's not absolutely definite.'

'Oh, I think it is. A certain Mr Green is on the trail.'

This was no time for playing silly.

'I've heard of him – just a while ago. He used to play cricket after a fashion. Brooke-Stanley told me about him.'

'Of course. Mr Green is looking forward to meeting you by the way.'

'I'm surprised he's not here,' I said rudely.

'Oh, but he is.'

Festing nodded amiably in the direction of a slim man with sandy hair, sitting at another table in the company of a shapely but hard-looking brunette.

'And that's his wife, I suppose?'

'Right. You haven't put a foot wrong.'

Mr Green smiled back and came over. Festing introduced us.

'I hope I'm not interrupting,' said Mr Green.

'Not a bit. I'm just going,' I said.

'What a pity. My wife would like to meet you.'

'Another time, I'm afraid.'

'We live in Kilburn,' said Mr Green, pointlessly I thought.

'That's handy. I hear you once played the game.'

'Still do, from time to time. I'm only forty-three, you know. That's about your age, isn't it?'

'It's in the record books.'

'You might turn out for us one Sunday, a charity game perhaps.'

'I think not.'

'Or open a fête?' suggested this horrible policeman.

I seized his hand as if to stop him talking. 'Well good night, Mr Green.'

'Good night, Mr Stenton. I will seen you soon, I hope.'

'Good night, Reg. See you tomorrow.'

And managing a curt nod to the staring Mrs Green, I escaped. But I was still in earshot when I heard Mr Green say, 'What a very nice chap.'

I plunged off furiously in the direction of Abbey Road and was nearly knocked down by a lad on a scooter (it was my fault) who swerved neatly to avoid me and called out, 'Watch it, dad!'

Julia and Polly were sitting down to supper in the big kitchen. Both were wearing housecoats that looked smart, crisp and new.

'You girls certainly put on the style,' I said, trying again to muster some reserves of good humour.

'Darling,' said Julia, getting up and kissing me on the cheek, 'what a pleasant surprise.'

I patted her cheek then did the same to Polly. 'Is the slave girl on duty? I want a huge gin and tonic with ice and lemon and served in the most elegant glass.' I had taken only one sip of the monster drink Festing had waiting for me. Perhaps Mrs Green was knocking it back.

'Polly. You heard what the man said.'

And Polly pleasantly and obediently did as she was told.

I smiled mechanically at Julia.

'Darling, you're miles away,' she said.

And so I was. Perhaps I had sex on the brain but now I was thinking that not only had both these women slept with Fitzgerald but had probably slept with one another as well. Julia, I knew, was a sleep walker and a sexual predator with a very keen and devious appetite. I had always felt that she was in need of help but that she was a most volatile and dangerous substance which needed handling with great care. I know she sensed in me a lack of understanding and a fear of her and that, to do her justice, she did her best by the lights of her own morality to cope with and even to protect me from strain and bewilderment. I could be wrong about Polly, of course, but she had an air of need and vulnerability that might put her at the mercy of the driving powers of either sex. But, in addition, like so many people who seem weak there was a hint that she might make capital out of it. Her 'innocence' had yet to be established.

'Here's your drink, Jack,' she said.

'Thank you very much. Would you excuse me while I make a couple of calls.'

Julia, setting a place for me, said, 'Don't go on all night.'

Francis answered the phone. 'Yes, Mr Stenton. Would you wait a moment.'

Brooke-Stanley came on promptly. 'Philip, I'm at Julia's and about to have supper. And I'm tired. Can it . . . can it wait until tomorrow? I shall have lots of time then.'

'Certainly. Ralph Stiell is coming to lunch. Join us before one, if you will.'

'Thank you. Are you coming to Julia's party, by the way?'

'Oh yes, I'll be looking in. I always enjoy Julia's parties. Good night.'

I rang Willie. He was still toiling. Although I felt like screaming, listening once again to the same old words tumbling from my mouth, I repeated the substance of the talk with Smith, not only to avoid any possible misunderstanding but also to be fair to Smith.

'The lad is doing his best,' I said.

'Aye,' said Willie cheerfully, 'but I'm not too sure about you. Not the cricket, of course; that's fair enough, if only fair. I've fiddled with the Fitzgerald piece a bit. It needed cheering up, if you know what I mean.'

'That I do,' I agreed heartily. 'Now are you coming to Julia's do tomorrow night?'

'I haven't been asked?'

'Oh yes, you have. And bring your missus too. About nine. If you must talk to me before then, you know where to find me. And now good night, for God's sake.'

'That didn't take long,' I announced, sitting down at table and finishing my gin. 'I've asked Willie and his wife to look in tomorrow. Is that all right?'

'Perfectly,' Julia poured our Chablis. 'There was a funny little news item on the telly tonight.'

'About Fitzgerald, I suppose?'

'Yes. Did he fall or was he pushed. That sort of thing.'

I looked at Julia with exasperation. 'He was pushed – you know that by now.'

Julia nodded. 'Perhaps you'll join us for coffee when you've finished your supper?' she said as she left the kitchen with Polly.

I joined them a little later, having decided that it was time for me to speak, to tell them, at some risk perhaps, almost all I knew. In short, I told them that the police were about to investigate the death of Fitzgerald with the view that he had been murdered. I told them about Mr Green. And I told Polly that if she had had a very recent and intimate association with the dead man then it would certainly come to light and she should decide, at once, a course of action and that almost certainly with legal advice. And further, that as a very good-looking and well-endowed young woman who enjoyed the company of cricketers, she would be a gift from heaven for the popular press – or any old press for that matter.

They listened in silence, through the haze of Julia's chain-smoking screen. Then Polly thanked me quietly and said she would like to talk to Julia about it. That was fine, I said, but once again I advised swift action. I then announced my intention of having a shower and going to bed. And I said good night and left them.

In my clean pyjamas (I had completely forgotten the suitcase that Peggy was leaving for me with Corker) I left the bathroom and headed for the bedroom. The bed looked cool and inviting. My foot caught something on the carpet by the dressing table. It was Julia's handbag and some of the contents spilled out. I bent down to put them back. Then between my fingers I first felt, then saw, a shiny postcard. It was a view of Nottingham Castle. I turned it over. In type-script on the back was the second message to Fitzgerald that Brooke-Stanley had described to me. 'Don't play at Lord's or you will wake up dead.'

I don't remember falling asleep or Julia coming to bed. When I awoke I could see her stretched beside me, wearing a white cotton nightdress that looked as stiff as a shroud. There was an incredible stillness about the place, disturbed only by her faint but regular breathing.

Saturday

The third day of a five-day Test Match is often the hinge on which the game swings, or creaks. It was true of that Saturday at Lord's. The game was laid open and exposed, with Sunday intervening before the final stages of the operation (weather permitting) on the Monday and Tuesday. When I had played in Test Matches I had always vaguely disliked these Sunday rest days. I had found them anything but restful, no matter how strenuous the previous three days' cricket had been. I was always a poor subject for relaxation. Even George Abbott, a man who loved to get his boots off and his feet up, did not usually relish this traditional break. Abbott might be taking a very different view this weekend, but I doubted it. He was a very stubborn and conservative man.

Saturday was not entirely a day off for me. True, I was free of copy dread and copy pressure, but the following afternoon I was required to file an analysis of the major incidents and trends of the first three days' play, for the enlightenment of our Monday morning readers. It was my job to get things in perspective and suggest – or rather, from the paper's angle, stick my neck out and say – who was going to win. I always hated this bit. It was invariably the stage when you had to eat most of the words you had written before the game had started. If the weather had intervened you were lucky. Mostly these predictions were – if you'll forgive me – hit and miss affairs. Either a powerful batting side, say, crumbled quietly away; or a side that was known to lack penetration in attack, shot out the opposition before the tea interval. And always, waiting to make nonsense of all predictions, was the pitch itself. That pitch which was asserted to be fast and lasting would, after flattering to deceive for a few early overs, prove listless in the long run. But with an England batsman retired hurt, and an Australian bowler dead, the copy would be expected to flow copiously. This didn't remove the act of crystal ball-gazing but, the human drama apart, some purely cricketing pros and cons would have to be made. I mention this because it is only the cricket that liberates my memory and sets me free to write about the other things. The cricket was the talisman, the touch-stone of the whole affair at Lord's.

These were my waking thoughts in Julia's bed. I touched her but she recoiled drowsily and I got up and went to the bathroom and threw open the window to let in some more hot weather. I showered and shaved and dressed (glad to accept the new shirt that was still waiting for me) and went into the deserted kitchen to make coffee. Soon Julia wandered in half-naked and asked me why Polly wasn't up yet. I managed one of those blank uncompromising glances that are calculated to provoke maximum irritation. It seemed to succeed for she hissed like a snake, refused coffee and rattled the unwashed dishes in the sink. I suggested that she might feel better and certainly look a lot more attractive if she had a bath and got dressed. She swept out and a moment later I heard her bawling at Polly. I went into the sitting room, lugging with me the awful burden of the day's papers. I scattered them on the sofa. The Test Death Mystery was building up in spite of a wall of silence and no-comment from England and Australian cricket spokesmen, the cricketers themselves, and medical authorities. Someone had discovered that Fitzgerald had a married sister living in Sydney. The only information from her was that she had seen little of her brother in recent years and that, as a boy, he had preferred tennis to cricket. They had always been a devout Catholic family and his body would be flown home for burial. And a former Australian Test captain was quoted as saying that Fitzgerald was the greatest all-rounder since Miller and Sobers and probably the fastest left-handed bowler in the history of the game. My own copy in terms of the pure cricket seemed fine and read very well. My Fitzgerald piece, sharpened up by Willie & Co., was adequate and informative but – or so it seemed to me – failed to depict Fitzgerald in convincing terms either as man or cricketer. But there would be more to come on that score. I believed that Fitzgerald's spirit was not one that would rest easily. He had not done with us yet. Nor perhaps had Inspector Green. There was a reference to him, not only as the officer in charge of the inquiries into Fitzgerald's death, but also as a lover, keen observer and (minor) player of the game. Meanwhile the England captain, Abbott, was reported to have a split skin, a sore head, mild concussion but no fracture and would be spending Saturday at home watching the Test on television before he returned to the fray on Monday. I rang his home.

Abbott answered immediately. His gritty response softened slightly when he knew who was calling. We were very different people but quite good friends. But he was cautious this morning and assumed the role of a friendly bank manager who was determined not to give you an overdraft.

'George, I hate to humour you but this is a simple inquiry after your health.'

'Better than the other fellow's, I'd say.'

'What happened to you?' I risked. It was a technical question.

'I made a balls of it, of course. Any fool could see that. Where were you at the time?'

I decided on silence. After a while he said, 'Jack, you had a better technique than me and just as much guts but the main difference was that you were a lucky bugger into the bargain. You would have blinked at the vital moment, and opened your eyes to find it had missed you. Mind you, I could have killed the bastard in that split second, you know, but I was calm enough when I came round. Poor sod.'

'George, don't ring off until I've finished the question but –?'

'I'll finish the question for you, Jack. They think Fitzgerald was murdered. Well, it could be. A copper called Green is coming round to see me. Now piss off, I'm having my breakfast. I'll see you on Monday.'

Through the door and the wall I heard a sarcastic screech from Julia followed by a wail – but with a note of defiance from Polly. I wondered if Julia was beating Polly up or merely giving her an impatient clout but I resisted the temptation to bear witness and for some strange reason decided to ring Festing. There was no reply. Then, equally without reason – or so it seemed to me – I rang Brooke-Stanley. I was relieved when Francis told me he was in the bath. Was it urgent or could it wait till lunch? Yes, it could. Francis knew everything. I then decided that the telephone was against me this morning and resolved to break its resistance with another call. I rang Peggy and asked her how she was and how the children were. They were all fine.

'Are you having a bad time, Jack?'

'What do you mean?'

'You sound distraught.'

'Rubbish.'

'Well, uncertain then.'

'Well, maybe,' I replied, trying to sound like my old candid, unconvincing self.

'Thanks for the cheque. Did you get the suitcase?'

'Yes,' I lied. 'Did you buy the coat?'

'No. I bought some underclothes and a pair of shoes.'

'I hope you had enough money,' I said.

'Not quite. You owe me fifteen pounds.'

I tried not to laugh, and failing, produced a sarcastic chuckle.

'Was there anything else?' she inquired after a long pause.

'No. Why?'

'The doorbell's ringing.'

'Then don't keep it waiting.' And I put the phone down.

Polly came in wearing a pale-blue dressing gown that was

open to reveal outlandish matching pyjamas (her own for sure) that clung to her with a sense of authority. She looked very self-possessed but one side of her face (not made-up) looked pinker than the other. Perhaps there had been a clout after all.

'Julia says will you come to breakfast?'

She turned and went out and after a moment I followed her.

Julia was smoking. She was wearing a filthy old négligée I had never seen before. A film of sweat on her upper lip suggested either lust or bad temper – possibly both. It was a mournful breakfast and given to accidents. Polly made toast, burning it in the process, and then knocked her coffee over. There was silence as she mopped it up. Then a faint, insistent hammering came from the flat beneath. I walked out and went back to the sitting room. I opened *The Times*, at random, and began to read a massive obituary of a dead German general.

I had a vision of another torrid June, that of 1941, and the din, dust and confusion as German armoured columns clattered over the plains of eastern Poland, but my thoughts were not supporting the picture in my mind's eye and it faded to be replaced by a postcard of Nottingham Castle. What was Julia doing with that, the visible proof of the President's story? I could only assume that Fitzgerald had given it to her. But it was serious and deadly evidence – Julia knew that. Why was it slopping around in her handbag? It should have been destroyed or at least kept in a very safe place. It was hardly the time to ask Julia about it. Moreover, she was at all times a private, secretive person and would hardly appreciate my explanation of disturbing her personal belongings.

It was an unprofitable situation and in the end, I reflected, might be almost as disastrous as Hitler's invasion of Russia. I returned to *The Times* and envied the skilful assembly of the facts and the events and the people, that fully justified the length of the piece. There was a sustained note of sardonic detachment rounded off with a modest flourish at the bottom of the column; the general, in the bosom of his family, had died in bed at his home in Bavaria.

Julia came in. She had certainly got a move on and was wearing my favourite dress. It was silk, in black and white vertical stripes with long sleeves, and stopping just about the knee. This morning it had been her turn to attack the champagne (Bollinger non-vintage, as usual) and she handed me one of the two glasses she was carrying and then sat down showing a lot of leg.

I was aware of an erotic peace-offering and said, coarsely, 'Watch your legs.'

She flicked at her dress and the thighs disappeared.

'Are you free for lunch?' she asked.

'No, I'm lunching with Philip and Ralph Stiell.'

'That will be nice. Perhaps you'll learn something for a change.'

I almost blurted it out and asked her if she'd read any good postcards lately, but she had introduced that old familiar tension again, setting the sexual machinery in motion and then frustrating it. Not for the first time I was aware of huge pressures building up inside her and crying out for release. But, as always, she seemed to convert her own frustrations into mine.

Julia looked at her watch. 'I have to call at the delicatessen in the High Street. If you can hang on a bit and help to shift some furniture, you might come out with me and we can have a drink before the cricket.'

'Right,' I said, and went back to the newspaper.

Polly, whose wardrobe (could it all be hers?) now seemed inexhaustible, came in again wearing a pink trouser suit. She stood obediently, like a maid or a younger sister, while Julia gave her instructions.

'Can you remember all that?'

'Of course.'

'Perhaps you'd better write it down.'

Polly scowled at Julia and smiled at me – a feat she

appeared to perform simultaneously. As she went out she passed Mrs Gates on her way in. Yet another sartorial revelation. Mrs Gates was wearing an old dress of Julia's, one that matched the colour of the green eyes. She had new, neat, matching shoes and looked smart and elegant. They drifted off into the kitchen. I was still reflecting on a woman's incessant need to look beautiful and different and yet always to be in fashion when they came back and summoned me to work. After moving furniture in the sitting room and in the dining room adjoining, and lugging around considerable quantities of champagne and other drinks too numerous to mention, we decided that the basic layout for the evening party was satisfactory; and just after ten I left the flat with Julia.

In the High Street we called at a shop or two, cashed cheques with Julia's newsagent and then went to a pub in Newcourt Street, a few steps from the police station. We drank tomato juice in silence until Julia said, 'Tell me some more.' This was a familiar request for stimulus and information, and I replied, 'Well, I spoke to Abbott this morning.'

'How is he?'

'A bit grumpy, but in good shape, I'd say.'

'Did he mention Fitzgerald?'

'Sort of,' I said warily. 'He certainly mentioned our friend, Green. He's paying a call on Abbott this morning. Bowl him a few full tosses, I expect.' Julia went quiet again. A man came in and I recognized him as the old member I had seen pottering among the gravestones on the Thursday morning. He gave me a stiff courteous nod and I responded.

'Who's that?' asked Julia.

'No idea, but now that I think of it, he reminds me of my dear old dad.'

Julia frowned and made an impatient gesture. Perhaps we had strayed onto dangerous ground. But then she said, 'Jack, have you ever thought of marrying me?'

It was my turn for frowning and impatience but I controlled myself and used delaying tactics.

'I've thought of leaving you,' I said.

'Oh I know that,' she said scornfully, 'but have you thought of leaving your wife?'

'For you?'

'Who else?'

Then I spoke the truth, a little too soon perhaps.

'Yes, I have thought of leaving Peggy and marrying you. It could hardly be worse than the absolute hell of living with you off and on. But Peggy doesn't believe in divorce, you know that.'

'For the sake of the children?'

'Now, now. You know better than that.'

'Oh, I know she loves you, if that's what you mean. You're weak. She knows you need her. She's in a very strong position.'

I wasn't rising to that one and replied, 'Just how strong are you?'

She laughed. 'I'm as strong as death . . . most of the time.'

'I don't understand you.'

'There's not a lot there,' she said, speaking to me but talking of herself. 'I must say I love sleeping with you. It gives me an incredible sense of power and, almost, fulfilment. Sometimes I think that, with a little care and encouragement, I might make a very good wife.'

She put her hands behind her head and turned away slightly. I recalled the nude sleep-walker pausing outside Polly's bedroom.

I was about to say something shattering, thought better of it, then promptly said it after all. 'Have you made love to any women?'

She turned to face me and fixed me with a long stare, friendly and encouraging, as if trying to draw me into the depths of her eyes.

'Well, yes, I have, a little. Were you thinking of Polly?'

'Yes.'

'Polly and I have made love.' Her eyes were perfectly still. 'Does that disturb you?'

'Yes,' I said.

'Does it excite you as well?'

I looked down into my empty glass.

'I'm going to drink a little gin,' I said, 'will you join me?'

'Certainly. Let me get them.'

The drinks came. She sipped hers and said, 'Now then, just a little of the truth game will do no harm.'

I gulped rather than sipped. 'Yes, I must confess it does excite me a little. And it fills me with despair as well.'

She lit a cigarette and I reached out and put my hand on hers.

'You're trembling,' I said.

'So are you.'

I gripped her very tightly indeed. Her eyes were now totally dark and without expression. 'What is it like?' I asked.

She smiled, but with her mouth only. 'It's awful,' she replied, 'but other nymphomaniacs may disagree.'

Now she had stopped trembling and some expression had flowed back into the front of her eyes.

I didn't know what to say but then these words came out of my mouth, 'Your eyes are green like a sea is green, sometimes light, sometimes dark, sometimes in between.'

'Green for danger just the same,' she said. 'Now that you're in a romantic mood, let's go and make love. I have the key to Linda's place. If she's out, that's fine; if she's in, it doesn't matter. There's tons of room.'

Linda lived in Primrose Hill. She had a huge flat.

'No,' I said, 'No. Wait, wait a bit.'

'All right,' she said cheerfully, 'I'll wait, then.'

'Do you need any help?' I said with a touch of desperation.

'What kind of help?'

'Are you involved in the murder of Fitzgerald?' I blurted out.

'Don't ask silly questions.'

'Well, let me help anyway.'

'You've just turned me down.'

'Julia, Julia,' I said with bitterness and reproach.

Suddenly she switched off her eyes and came out of her trance. She stood up and walked out into the street. I followed her.

'I must get back and help Eileen,' she said. 'Have a good lunch. Give my love to Philip and say I look forward to seeing him later. Look in at tea-time, if you feel like it. If not, don't stay boozing too long after the end. I shall need your manly strength and tact. Drag Reg along with you. Try not to be late. Some nice girls have been invited but, on balance, they'll be in short supply.'

She kissed my cheek and left me, moving swiftly and sinuously like a cat does when it has made up its mind.

I walked to Lord's, apologized to Corker for forgetting to collect the case and went to the Press Box. The weather was much as before, the atmosphere heavier if anything and the light hazy.

Australia, with Madden and Musgrave, resumed at 255 for 3. Just before lunch (at 1.27 to be precise) they were all out for 355. Ackroyd took one wicket and the 'ageing' fast men, Mappleton and Standish, shared the other five. They simply kept the ball well up and it swung to and fro like a pendulum. As Mappleton said to me afterwards (affecting bad grammar just to annoy me), 'We was bowling well above our class.' I hastened to agree with him but added, charitably, that I was glad I wasn't batting. It was the type of bowling that had always bothered me. I also made a mental note to tell Musgrave – a quite superb cricketer in that jaunty, yet ruthless, Australian vein – that he must learn to keep his head still. I should add that the spinner, Flinders, one of those small men who seem to carry a bat far too big for control and comfort, hit Ackroyd for two staggering sixes into the Mound Stand; and that with Fitzgerald dead the Australians were now for the duration of the game reduced to ten batsmen.

I left Lord's just before one to be in time for lunch with

Brooke-Stanley. His front door was open as usual and Francis was standing at the threshold.

'The President is still at the cricket, sir.'

'Is he?' I was slightly annoyed.

'The television is on, sir. A very good picture of the cricket, if I may say so.'

'No, no. Not that.'

'In that case, sir, perhaps you would like to join Dr Stiell? He's in the garden.'

'Perhaps I'd better do that,' I said reluctantly.

'Now what would you care to drink, sir? We have opened the Chablis.'

'Thank you. I'll settle for a pink gin, if I may.'

And I passed through the house and into the garden.

Dr Ralph Stiell was about sixty and had been in fashionable practice for almost thirty years. He was what is still called an eminent physician and looked the part, silver hair, slim, dapper and all the rest of it. He had also acquired a new young wife, a born shrew with a figure that would have started a riot in a blizzard given sufficient exposure. But she seemed a frigid bitch. I had known Stiell for many years and the mutual dislike that was joined at our first meeting had not altered one jot. My father, who had known him well, had described him as the perfect blend of an upstart and a snob. I had settled for that without protest. Stiell was courteous to the point of impertinence but I never needed lessons in this field. And I also knew from observation, hearsay, and some experience that he was a very good doctor. His cricketing expertise was another matter. He had, you might say, watched the game without looking at it, talked to those who played the game without listening to them, and was lamentably ignorant of its basic laws. Even his manners creaked noticeably. He stood up to greet me with a considerable show of reluctance and eyed me with that suave, professional aplomb of a specialist about to deal with a recalcitrant patient.

'Ah . . . er Jack . . .' he said, nearly making it Jock.

'Ralph,' I replied firmly. He liked to be known as 'Rafe'.

We sat there uncomfortably in the heat. Francis came out with the gin for me and refilled Stiell's glass with the President's Chablis. For a moment I thought that the silence between us might harden into a pact, or truce, until the President arrived but Stiell began a rambling dissertation on cricket, a sort of Thirtle-like disquisition but without the latter's knowledge and information. I was in no mood for this and broke in abruptly, saying, 'How about the inquest on Fitzgerald?'

He looked annoyed and said, 'I'm not sure about that.'

'Not sure, or won't say?'

Stiell looked appalled yet dignified, to show that his medical ethics were not to be trifled with.

'These things take time . . . there are certain tests . . . one must be thorough and above all sure before . . .'

His voice trailed off and he looked hopefully over his shoulder in search of the President. He was not disappointed. Brooke-Stanley was advancing nimbly over the lawn.

There was a gleam in his eye and he said. 'Sorry to be late. I hope you've broken the ice?'

'On the contrary,' I replied, 'we were just beginning to skate on hot water.'

The President patted my shoulder in soothing fashion. 'There now. Wherever did you find that phrase?'

'Ah, that would be telling.'

Then we went in to lunch.

For a time we were back with the cricket again. But the President, fortunately, was in a wicked mood. He refused for a while to be drawn on the issues at hand and delved into the past: 'Well, as you know, Prince Ranjitsinhji not only said that "cricket is a game which keeps boys out of mischief", he also said that "it makes individual men life-long friends". Now there's a text for the Sunday morning sermon. And don't forget Lord Harris. He went one better with: "You do well to love cricket, for it is more free from anything sordid, anything dishonourable, than any game in the world" . . . How about that, then?' And the old man sat back and roared with laughter.

But the mood changed when I got down to brass tacks again. I went through the old routine. Stiell started spluttering but the President waved him to silence.

'Now Ralph, you know that Fitzgerald died of poison, or a massive overdose of some stimulant, or whatever. I don't know, or need to know, the details – they'll all come out in the wash. Now either he did this thing, or these things, to himself, or someone else was responsible. Accident can almost certainly be ruled out. So it's either suicide or murder. Do you agree?'

Stiell winced. 'Well, I suppose so . . . but –'

'We will deal with the buts, Ralph. Your cagey professionalism is no great help in these matters. Has Mr Green spoken to you yet?'

'Really, Philip . . .'

'He has, then. And to you, Jack?'

'Yes. I thought you said I would like him.'

'He's a great admirer of yours,' said the President with a sardonic chuckle.

'Balls.'

'Very appropriate, I must say. But don't write off Green. He is a very shrewd and sophisticated type of policeman. I have the highest regard for him. And who knows, his knowledge of cricket may come in very handy. But to go on, may I say that the murderer – and I am convinced that there *is* one – is a cricketer, and, to be precise, a cricketer who is a member of one of the two sides playing in the present Test Match – here at Lord's,' he added, with a flourish.

'Including the twelfth men?'

'Why not? Why not? A distinct possibility.'

At this stage the Chablis had been succeeded by Montrachet. The old boy was knocking back this powerful, sometimes gamey and acidulous wine with great gusto. I marvelled at his constitution and his digestion.

But I was not so impressed by his flashes of insight that seemed to me to be more of a hindrance than a help, nor by his moments of mischief and intrigue when he appeared to be playing a game with some very dangerous materials. Not all old people are foolish all the time, but many of them are some of the time. I had a suspicion that what for him had begun as a very serious matter was now being blurred by his frivolity. He had become too pleased with himself. He was vain, that was it.

'Let's get back to Green for a moment,' I said. 'The police, in fact. You seem to have a high opinion of the Inspector. I dare say you're right. I'm no great judge of character. So can we take it, then, Philip, that you have taken him entirely into your confidence, that very properly you have told him in detail all that you know and suspect – indeed all that you've told *me* – and that he's now fully in the picture, or one might say, the picture-*postcard* picture?'

This meant nothing to Stiell who looked quite baffled but stayed silent. If the President got the point then he gave not the slightest impression of having done so. Indeed he retreated promptly into absent-mindedness.

'Yes, it's to do with the cricket, you see,' (again that cryptic and infuriating reference) 'but it would be silly to rush things . . . one must be sure . . . all in good time.'

He tailed off and I spoke out rudely.

'You're just as bad as Ralph here. And you have the nerve to call him cagey.'

Stiell wriggled in his chair and the President sat bolt upright in his. His cheeks were now flushed red with the white wine, and perhaps a little anger too, but he restrained himself, then gathering himself together with the confidence of the fine striking clock in the corner, said, 'Do be patient, Jack. You know you are my sole confidant –'

'No, I don't know, and if I am I'd rather I wasn't.'

'Ralph's a bit of a coward,' he went on amazingly, 'but at least he knows his job and can bear witness.'

'Now what on earth do you mean by that?' I snapped.

He answered this by speaking to Ralph. 'Sorry about that, Ralph, it must have sounded rather rude.'

Stiell made a most curious movement appearing both to nod and shake his head at the same time.

I stood up. 'Thank you for an excellent lunch, sir,' I said formally. He responded by shaking my hand. 'It's a pleasure, my boy. I'll see you tonight at Julia's party.'

'Good-bye, Ralph,' I said, 'you've been a great help, I must say.'

I left them at the table.

Back from lunch I stayed at Lord's until the end of play. England began their second innings with a show of relief at being only 132 runs behind. Hindmarsh and Eyre opened the Australian attack. It was grim stuff and I could only hope that Fitzgerald would get a last laugh out of it. At the close, with Branston and Byron together, England were 150 for 1, for the loss of Jarvis. It was the one day that the cricket and the heat matched one another in tedium. Bowlers came and went but batsmen didn't. Everyone seemed to be trying but the side in the field, though missing nothing, appeared incapable of creating chances. The batsmen, instead of taking advantage, settled for a quiet life. It seemed a poor exhibition for a capacity crowd, but they were quiet enough under the circumstances, resigned perhaps to the fact that a five-day Test Match (and this one in particular) needs a quiet passage before the onset of any final feverish crisis.

It is hard to say why the Australian batting had collapsed on a wicket that the England openers found tolerably easy to cope with. Leaving aside the tendency of cricket reporters to find reasons when there are none, to imply cunning when there is only toil and patience, I can only suggest that at certain periods of any cricket match the fortunes of batsmen and bowlers ebb and flow more by the law of averages than the conditions. It is not so much a mystery as an observable fact.

The party piece – Julia's – started at eight and ended at

two in the morning. There were some bad consequences, indeed all the horrors that followed seem to have gathered force there. It was a staging post for disaster. It was throughout a tough, tense and crowded affair in the context of very heavy drinking by virtue of abundant supplies. But as far as Julia's flat was concerned there was no violence, very little horse play and scarcely any barrack room damages. There were some sharp edges, of course, but the innuendo and the sexual cut and thrust must be seen as a natural consequence of the people present. There must have been at least seventy but the core was England and Australian cricketers and their wives and girlfriends. The rest were journalists, personal friends (of Julia's) and a modest, mild gate-crashing fringe.

There was no music, thank God, but the noise and the heat of human beings on a very hot night in a confined space has never failed to arouse in me a feeling of utter joylessness. There are always too many people. But without music and dancing and jiggling and joggling, people do happily tend to settle in groups. At least you can move around. I had promised to circulate, but at once was cornered by a small, dark, pretty girl called Angie. She talked very intently of the joys of the three-day event and a horse that her father had bought her called Doomsday. At this early stage with others still to come, it was still quiet and clear enough (the smokers not fully extended) and with open spaces and passages between people to take in the scene without effort. Julia was chatting to Hindmarsh, Festing to Hunt and Mrs Gates was getting on well with Kirkstead. Through a gap I caught sight of Polly and Byron. Byron had good manners as well as looks and great charm and was trying them all out on Polly. Polly as usual was trying out herself. She had produced a mini-dress that brought out the best in all of her as she sat perched on the edge of a fragile table. It was almost too much to bear; those harmonious curves, the calves acknowledging the knees on the way to the thighs, then the waist and the opulent bosom, firm but flowing, the heavy but majestic shoulders and finally the graceful neck supporting a round desirable head you could play football with.

'What an attractive girl,' said Angie brightly as she followed my gaze.

'You must meet Mr Byron,' I replied and dragged her off to break it up.

I gripped Byron's arm. He smiled graciously as I took Polly away to another corner of the room. I pretended not to see the hungry looks directed at Polly by the three young Turks from New South Wales, Maitland, Madden and Musgrave. But they seemed tolerably happy with three of Julia's mercenaries, all very nice girls who could be as tough as old boots, if necessary. They might well need to be, I thought. In the background, by the door to the hall, I heard the voice of Brooke-Stanley. He was holding court and proclaiming the genius of Maurice Tate. Then Thirtle, getting a word in edgeways with the President, and the squawky, bossy tones of Dr Stiell's wife, Muriel.

Polly was a little tight already. At any rate she put one hand on my shoulder while she drank champagne with the other. 'I must circulate,' she said, like a child recalling a basic directive. 'Julia will be after me.'

I turned round to catch, of course, Julia's mocking eye. Somehow she had managed to land Angie with Flinders and was talking herself to Byron who had just lit a very fine-looking cigar.

'Don't be afraid,' I said boldly to Polly.

'If you're going to start about Fitzgerald again,' she replied with equal directness but in a zombie-like voice, 'Julia says that it's best to wait and see what happens.'

That didn't sound quite like Julia. 'I don't agree with her,' I said flatly.

She pouted and stretched back, then glanced down at her terrific leg-flow. 'Please don't try to make me, Jack. I wouldn't mind, but Julia would give me hell. And you too, I suppose,' she added gently.

I could have hit her. Then for the first time I looked very

closely into her eyes. The pupils were dilated. She took her hand from my shoulder and took me by the wrist.

'Now, let go, Polly. People are looking at us. And one of them is bound to be Julia.'

'I don't care,' she said illogically. 'Do you?'

'Listen, Polly, just for a moment. It's very important. Did Fitzgerald give you anything, anything at all that would interest the police?'

'No. You heard that the other day when Julia asked me, especially for your benefit.'

'Why should she do that?'

'Perhaps she's taken pity on you,' she giggled and looked stupid.

Now I knew why Julia had an urge – probably succumbed to – to clout her occasionally.

'I only slept with Fitzgerald twice, you know. I know very little about him.' I began to realize that in some ways this woman was quite impregnable. I went on trying.

'Polly,' I said sharply, 'just listen for once. Whoever killed Fitzgerald will have to kill again –'

'Why?' she broke in.

'Oh they do, they always do.' I did not sound convincing. She shrugged.

'He was very kind to me,' she said suddenly.

'I give up,' I said.

And then she said in a burst, 'He told me that Hunt had a grudge against him and that someone put me up to going to bed with him.'

'Well?'

Polly swayed slightly. 'I was very upset about that,' she said. 'Nobody tells me who to sleep with.'

Then as expected Julia came boring in, bringing with her Hunt, Lytton, Flinders, my Sports Editor, Willie, and his very practical wife, Janet. It was all smooth enough, but confusing in the way that all those conversations at all those gatherings inevitably are. I began a conversation of my own with Hunt, then someone dropped and broke a glass and the moment was lost. I took the opportunity to help Mrs Gates carry the debris into the kitchen. When I came back I bumped into Forester. The MCC Secretary was a bachelor with a roving eye but very cautious in his approach. He was practical and ambitious and ran a very efficient office. It struck me idly, as he smiled at me, that he would have made a first-class England captain had he gone on to a county after university. Sadly he was but one of many talented stylists who had rejected the meagre rewards of the game.

Forester grabbed two glasses from the passing Mrs Gates who had now thoroughly captivated and put to work the amiable Kirkstead who gave me a heavy optimistic wink as he followed her along. Forester then asked me if, as a very special friend of Brooke-Stanley's, I had noticed anything odd about him lately. Since the game began, that was. I replied in a pompous stilted manner that I had noticed nothing odd at all and could only describe the President's behaviour in terms of a renewed zest for life, arising probably out of the misfortunes of others.

'He's very cantankerous,' said Forester, 'and rather secretive and tiresome at the moment.'

'Certainly he shouldn't use your office,' I said shortly.

'Oh, I don't mind that. It's difficult to let go when you're getting on a bit.'

'Don't look at me,' I said. 'What's *your* next step forward?'

He spread his arms carefully, taking care not to spill his drink. 'What indeed? You tell me.'

'You can wait for dead man's shoes,' I said evenly. 'But be sure you choose the right size.'

Forester gave me an old-fashioned look, then we were swept back into the room. Forester, I reflected, would make an ideal murderer, especially at Lord's where he knew all the ropes. I looked at him, almost fondly, in this light, but it seemed far too good – and too simple – to be true.

The talk-level had risen and the atmosphere thickened. It was extremely warm and the lights were low. It was becoming increasingly difficult to move around without squeezing and shoving a little. The weak (and in some cases the sensible) were being pinned in corners. Drinks and glasses became confused but everyone was still drinking. The fit cricketers were punishing Julia's abundant supplies of champagne. I observed that the three batsmen from New South Wales, rather like a hunting party, had settled on their prey. Arrangements were being made. Then Willie and Janet got across to me. They lived miles away and were about to leave. Willie took the opportunity to discuss the copy for Monday. That didn't take long.

'Any news on the other front?' asked Willie.

'No. How's Smith and brothers getting on?'

'Slowly. Smith is out of it now. He kept confusing Byron with Lyndhurst and mistook Reg Festing for the President of MCC.'

'Sounds promising. You should have kept him at it.'

'Reg is pretty high, by the way,' said Willie.

'What's he drinking?'

'Whisky.'

'And you?' I asked.

'The same, of course. Now –'

'Now that will do,' Janet Williamson intervened. 'Home, Willie boy.' Willie gave me a playful punch.

'Look out, you old sod. Take care.'

'Who's driving?' I asked.

'I am,' said the clear-eyed Janet. And they pushed away to take their leave of Julia.

Now Festing's voice, though coming from the dining room, was high above the din. Patiently I made my way through the crush. It was an interesting passage. Julia, looking relaxed and alert, was talking to Hunt and holding his hand in a casual way. Hunt caught my eye and made a most disagreeable face. I gave him a sweet smile and retained it for Byron who had his arm around a pretty girl I had not seen before. Hindmarsh was deep in a technical discussion with Standish, with Mappleton as a sceptical audience. By a window I caught Mrs Gates allowing Kirkstead a chaste and delicate kiss while keeping a firm hold on his hands. Polly was sitting down and talking to Angie, the horse girl, who stared in some amazement at the exposed thighs of her companion. Thirtle was cornered by Ransley and listening with impeccable politeness. Forester was drifting but I passed safely behind him.

In the dining room Festing was the centre of a group that contained Brooke-Stanley, Lyndhurst, Burnett, Eyre, Yarcombe and Ackroyd. He was drunk all right, but not hopelessly so and appeared to be having little trouble with his words and consonants. 'A man was telling me the other day that the amateur spirit was moribund. Moribund! I was glad to inform him that it had died years ago. It died with the war – do you know that? – along with all the other good things and many of the good people. Amateur spirit – there's no such thing any more. Look at our game, one of the last to fall, you could say, but look at it now. It's as bad as, if not worse than, the rest. The bloody game is being run by insurance companies, tobacco barons, booze tycoons, soft drink corporations – they're the worst of the lot – bread companies, clothing manufacturers and makers of trendy sports equipment. You name it and cricket's got it. As for the players, they don't play hard enough, or practise enough, and so, my friends, it stands to reason that they're just not bloody good enough! Where are the Gentlemen and the Players? Where are they now? Gone to bloody graveyards, every one. Will they ever learn? Of course they bloody well won't!'

Festing paused and actually mopped his brow, following that with a huge swig of the product of a distinguished distillery. Julia's whisky, need I say, was of the same excellence as the rest of her drink. Suddenly I felt pressure at my back. I glanced around. I had been joined by Julia, Hunt, Byron, Forester and Polly, among others. Through all this Brooke-Stanley appeared to be listening, or rather, as it struck me after, to be thinking. He was staring at the ceiling.

Festing's audience was tolerant, certainly more amused than convinced. Some raucous laughs and coarse asides had failed entirely to ruffle his composure. Perhaps he was deafened by his own words, but anyway he plunged on. 'And the modern game, as a spectacle, that is, is a crying shame and a disgrace. The way some of these chaps are bowling at the moment – yes, right here and now in this game at Lord's – why, you would think they had been given a licence to kill. In particular, I would –'

But here Festing was stopped abruptly and with magisterial authority by the MCC President. 'That's enough, Festing. Now shut up or get out – either will do. Both would be preferable.' Brooke-Stanley's voice, though not heavy, was piercing and with a deadly cutting edge.

There was complete silence. Festing turned to the President, opened his mouth and, much to my relief and astonishment, bowed his head in contrition. He said, 'I'm sorry, sir. Please forgive me. I was going too far.' Then with surprising dignity and steadiness he passed, still holding his glass, through the lane that had opened for him and went into the sitting room.

I followed him as the party got back into gear. These things happen at parties and are soon forgotten – well, sometimes they are. I found him in a chair by the window. He was sitting rather awkwardly and his eyes were wild, but he seemed reasonably self-possessed now, and still had a capable grip on his glass. I had drunk very little that evening. I found a clean glass and an open bottle and sat by Festing to drink a glass of champagne.

'Yes,' he muttered, sensing my presence but not looking at me, 'perhaps I shouldn't have said that, but it's true. It's a good job, though, I didn't go on . . .'

'Why?' I asked curiously.

It was just then that I became aware of some movement behind me. One, two or maybe three people. I still dream about that moment, dream that I looked around and saw, among the faces, just one very special face. But in fact I never looked round at all. I just bent forward to hear Festing's reply.

'Those bloody Australians,' and now his voice began to thicken, 'they're the worst of the lot. No manners, no morals, no civilization. Look at the way they treat their women for a start – their wives like dirt and their women much, much worse. They ought . . .'

This time I stopped him short. I shook him none too gently and he dropped his glass. Once again he reacted with surprising mildness.

'Don't worry,' he said, picking up his empty glass. 'I'll get another one. There's another thing, though, that's even more important. One thing leads to another, you know. Don't forget to read my copy in the morning.' And he stumbled away.

Before I could move I was joined by Thirtle, who, seemingly impervious to time, heat, heated talk, drink, sex, life and death, asked me quietly, as if we had been sitting in a club, if I would kindly read (in the near future) the outline of a book he was planning on the history of the great spin bowlers. This great art, he argued, embodied in the recorded performances of the supreme masters, was now (and here he did make a reference to Festing's outburst that showed he'd heard it after all) was much more moribund than the amateur spirit and would soon be as dead as the Latin language. I listened in astonishment but before becoming punch drunk I managed to say, 'For Christ's sake, Thirtle, who asked you to this party?'

'I did.' It was Julia and she patted Thirtle's balding head. 'The dear boy. Don't you think he'd be good for Angie, the sweet, petite little thing that she is.'

'Where's Festing?' I asked suddenly, getting to my feet.

'He's gone home. Quite a few people have gone home.'

'Not with Reg, I'll be bound. I should have gone with him, you know.'

I looked at my watch. It was 11.40.

'Don't fret,' said Julia, pushing Thirtle out of his chair

and taking his place. 'Old Reg has found his way home before when he's been much, much worse.'

'That's not the point,' I said aimlessly – or was it so aimless?'

I looked around. There were some open spaces now. Many had gone but a fair number remained. I saw the faces, the profiles and the backs of the heads but I quite failed to recognize them in terms of people I knew. I was looking without seeing, worried within about the absent Festing. Should I go after him?

'Excuse me,' I said to Julia, and I left the sitting room. To make absolutely certain I looked in the dining room, the hall and the kitchen and the bathroom. There was no sign of the old buzzard. He'd gone, all right. I paid a visit to the lavatory, calmed down a little and then went back to the sitting room. Julia had left her chair and was talking cheerfully to Burnett and Eyre and Stiell's wife who seemed in high, noisy spirits. There was no sign of her husband. Her ample but very firm flesh was tightly packed into a low-cut dress. Her white skin was gleaming brightly and she looked rather preposterous. Julia caught my eye and winked broadly. Suddenly I felt better. The panic had passed. I sat down by the window. I had had only a few sips of champagne and now I didn't fancy the taste at all. I poured myself a large whisky and added a generous measure of water. With any luck, no one would join me for a while.

Suddenly I heard the sitting room phone extension ring near me. As it rang I looked at my watch before answering. It was two minutes to midnight. No one else seemed to be aware of the phone and I snatched it up.

As I listened to the voice that was impersonal yet considerate, telling me the facts as far as they were known but being quite definite that a life was in the balance and that the subject was asking for me, I felt the chill of sweat on my brow. Looking across the dark room I met, inevitably, the eyes of the demon goddess, Julia. She cut through the throng like a laser beam and stood by me. I noticed a smudge of lipstick at the corner of her mouth and a small vein throbbing in her temple. I replied to the voice on the phone and rang off.

Julia touched me lightly over the heart.

'What's the matter?'

'It's Reg Festing.'

'What does he want?'

'He's been run over in Hamilton Terrace, just near his flat. He's in the ... the hospital down the road. That one. He's seriously injured and it seems he's asking for me, for me.'

Julia went very still and said, 'I see. Shall I come with you?'

'No.'

'One of the boys, perhaps?'

'No. Just keep it quiet.'

She walked with me to the door.

'Will you be back?'

'Of course. As soon as I can.'

'What knocked him down?' she asked through the narrowing gap of the door.

'A car. Hit and run.'

Sunday

Sunday was a day I had always disliked as a child and even at this early hour I was aware of the familiar onset of boredom and misery as I stepped out of the flat. In the street I paused and looked up at Julia's open windows. The light from them was subdued and the noise faint. Someone appeared to be watching me but the figure was blurred and moved quickly away before my gaze. I set off through the very hot night on the short walk to the hospital. In spite of some inward dread I felt well enough, with my head clear and my legs firm and supple. I suppose I was light-headed rather than light-hearted but as I stepped out briskly my anxiety was allayed, curiously enough, by the certain conviction that the person who had killed Fitzgerald had now tried to murder Festing. The possibility of an accident seemed infinitely remote.

The hospital was a great muddle of a place. Founded and built in the nineteenth century by a religious order and supported by charitable contributions on a reasonably lavish scale, it had been enlarged and modernized in the 1930s, and then in part torn down, rebuilt and extended in the 1950s. I had never been inside and though I must have passed the place hundreds of times I had difficulty in finding the entrance to Casualty. I discovered it, very difficult of access, in a small lane at the back. Outside there was a black saloon with a uniformed policeman at the wheel. He watched me closely as I went inside.

I was sure that Festing would still be nearer to the grave than the relative comfort of a bed in a ward. I had a vision of a stricken man, clothes torn and covered in blood, isolated in a pool of light and surrounded by figures performing some ordered and unhurried ritual. But as I entered the building I saw a trolley being vigorously propelled down a long and narrow corridor. As I focussed, the party made a sharp turn and vanished round a corner. It resembled a scene from a ludicrous hospital comedy of manners, complete with eccentric doctors, wild nurses and mad porters whizzing, like clowns on roller skates, up and down interminable passages in search of a vital but still unknown destination, with the patient flat on his back and resigned to his fate.

I stood in a small hall at the top of the long corridor. A small desk with telephone and books and pens suggested the place of a receptionist. But standing there was a young police constable. Before we could speak a bell rang stridently in the distance then stopped abruptly to give way to the muffled clang of ancient lift doors closing. Then a man came through a door a little way down the passage.

He was in his twenties, with a square, muscular frame, very strong features and jet-black hair. He bore an unnerving resemblance to the young Freddie Trueman.

'Mr Stenton.' There was no question, just a statement of fact. His voice was flat and so were his vowels. His handshake was warm but on the bone-crushing side. The Queen would not have welcomed it.

'My name is Spilsby. Dr Spilsby. Come into the office.'

I nodded to the policeman and followed the doctor whose white coat showed signs of the heat and stress of the day.

It was a small room with brown linoleum, a brown, scarred table littered with tinny ashtrays. There were some wonky-looking chairs. The impression was bleak and functional, though not without character. There was a hint of the President's broom cupboard at the rear of the pavilion. Spilsby looked very tired and very fit. He ripped open a pack of cigarettes and asked me to sit down.

'You didn't waste time,' he said. 'Do you smoke?'

'No. And I wasn't far away. It sounded urgent, even desperate.'

'Do you drink?' he asked.

'Yes.'

He lit his cigarette and went to a battered filing cabinet. He pulled out a bottle. 'It's whisky, filed under W. I haven't had one for twelve hours. Will you join me?'

'Gladly.' I made a mental note to replenish his supplies. Then he poured the stuff into very clean tumblers, went to a small sink in the corner and filled a jug with water.

I made my own, lifted the glass and said with a gesture of self-possession, 'Your very good health, Dr Spilsby. You talk and I'll listen.'

'That will save time,' he replied, and put his feet up on the table.

The room was amazingly cool.

'Now, Mr Festing – I know him by sight and that he lives nearby – has just gone to surgery. He may be lucky. One of our consultants, Mr Paulger, a brain surgeon, was just going home when your friend was admitted. Well, he's not going home just yet.'

Spilsby inhaled and drank some whisky.

'It's like this. Mr Festing has been run over and suffered severe injuries to the head and chest. I saw him first on admission. He was conscious then and immediately told me, quite clearly, your name and a phone number where we could reach you. That was that. His speech broke up and he became incoherent. Calls were then made to you and to the police. At the same time the man who brought Festing here went into mild shock and we had to deal with him too. It was difficult to stop him talking.'

Spilsby paused, probably out of politeness, to allow me to register.

'It seems that this man was in a car with his girlfriend in Hamilton Terrace. The car was parked without lights, not far from Abercorn Place. Festing distracted them slightly; they saw him hesitate before crossing the road. Then a car

– without lights – swept round the corner and knocked Festing down as he stepped off the curb. Then the driver stopped, reversed and deliberately ran over him. Then he drove forward, again over Festing's body, and went like a bat out of hell in the direction of Marble Arch. Then the man, the witness, started his car, drove up and with the help of the girl, it seems, dragged Festing into the back and brought him back here. Pretty quick thinking, all considered.'

I thought of the peculiar, though not insuperable, problems of making love in a car.

'Do people usually respond like this?' I asked feebly.

'This one did. You never can tell.'

'Where is he now?'

Spilsby swung his feet from the desk and jerked his head. 'Oh he's still around. Unlike your friend I think he'll be going home shortly. By the way, the place is stiff with policemen. They'll want to see you before you go. If you're detained more than two minutes, I'll be surprised. It's just the mere formality at work. I insisted on speaking to you first.' He brought the bottle over and poured out, very carefully, two very small measures. 'That's it then. One for the road for you, and one for the rest of the night for me. Cheers.' He went to the cabinet and restored the bottle to the file.

'I don't think,' he said, with a sympathetic glance, 'that I can tell you any more. I suppose I shouldn't be telling you this. And who knows, the witness may be telling a different story by now. They often do, when they've calmed down and are made to answer questions instead of putting things in their own way. As it happens,' Spilsby went on with a touch of sorrow and indiscretion, 'he's a local man, too, an estate agent, God rest his soul. He's married and the girl in the car with him was not his wife.'

We exchanged mournful glances. I was aware of a slight tug of fatigue. I stood up, finished the whisky and said, 'Thanks, very much, for your help and understanding. There's just one more thing, though. Did Festing say anything, anything at all, a word or a phrase perhaps, apart from telling you my name and the phone number?'

Spilsby responded by speaking to himself.

'Yes, now I come to think of it, it's a clear case of attempted murder.'

I wasn't disposed to argue with that and I waited to see if he would answer my question. He took a pen from his pocket and tapped his teeth with it. 'I can't be sure,' he said very slowly, then with a change of mind said very quickly, 'Yes, yes I can. He muttered something about fast bowling, and the words "dangerous", and possibly, "fear" came in somewhere. And that was all.'

'I see. And when might there be some more?'

'I don't know,' said the doctor, 'I just can't tell you that. But the police, as they say, will be in attendance.'

'You must have noticed that he'd been drinking?'

'Oh yes, indeed. He'd had a skinful, I'd say.'

'Does that matter?'

'Not necessarily. But he's got two bad ones, all right. One in the head, and one in the chest.'

I was thinking of something else to say when Spilsby briskly cut in.

'Now then, Mr Stenton, why don't you go home? No use hanging around here. There's nothing you can do.'

'You're right. I'll keep in touch.'

He came out into the passage with me.

'A funny business, this cricket match,' said the doctor. 'Was it a good party, by the way?'

'Not bad. It's probably still going on. Care to join me?'

'Alas, no. I'm quite fond of the game,' he said absently. 'But I don't know any cricketers.'

'Better keep it that way. And again, thanks a lot. I'll see you in church.'

Spilsby laughed and turned away as the policeman left his post by the desk and approached me with notebook in hand. I gave him some dreary details of my whereabouts and suggested that the police should ring Festing's paper. Someone ought to be told, though I had no idea if Festing had any living relatives. The policeman was very big and young and polite. I felt more old than tired and went out into the night. The police car had gone.

The lane at the back of the hospital was poorly lit and at least two of the street lamps were not working. I turned left to make the slightly longer walk this time to the main road at the end, but heading back in the direction of Julia's flat. The hospital buildings took up most of the lane on my left. There was a tiny pavement. On the right was a wall of medium height. It was of red brick and crumbling and skirted some tennis courts. There was no footway on this side and the wall was lined with plane trees at regular intervals. I walked along in their shadow. It was past one o'clock. Spilsby's whisky had done me no harm but somehow I was resisting the supreme effort required to think clearly about the latest stage of this game within a game. I remember having my hands in my pockets and my head down, giving an impression perhaps of a man trudging along without a thought for his surroundings. In fact I was in a highly alert, nervous state allied to that sensation of sheer physical well-being and exuberance that I first experienced as a boy when I was tying up my gym shoes before a game. There was that slight trembling of the fingers, the quickening of the pulse and what I can only call the supreme confidence of stage fright. It's what Bradman was trying to express. Words seem inadequate. Perhaps the total response would find its best expression in music. In a condition such as this all the senses tend to be extremely sharp and, in my case, especially the sense of hearing. Behind my back I heard a faint noise of pursuit. It was simultaneously the feather-like tread of the panther, the hiss of the blade, the soft deadly flap of the wings of the angel of death. It may appear easy to write this now but it's precisely what I felt then.

Even then, it was jerking my hands from my pockets that may have saved my life in the first place. This split-second reaction caused me to stumble and as I dropped on one knee the vicious, deadly descent of the club passed by my head and caught me an agonizing, paralysing but glancing blow on the top of my left arm. But it put me flat on my face and set me up perfectly for the next stroke. It was precisely at that moment that a light came on in a downstairs room of the hospital. The light rushed through the uncurtained window and seemed to explode in the dark street with me as its target. It seemed to me brighter than a thousand suns. Behind me I heard a startled intake of breath and when the club came down again it lacked its previous force. Twisting round I caught it with both hands, riding a blow that, though checked, might have smashed my wrist, and dragged it away. And the light in the window went out with the same immaculate timing of its coming on. But with the intensity of the light in my eyes and the searing pain in my arm I saw no one. No one at all, not even a shape, or the shape of a shape. I only heard the sound of the softest footsteps running away from me at great speed. Then silence. I clasped the club to me with the passion of a distraught child holding onto a favourite toy. The silence deepened, there was a wave of nausea, a struggle against darkness and oblivion, an awareness of not crying out, then the roots of the trees by the wall stopped swaying and the street stopped shaking and became still again. With the help of the club I got to my feet and stumbled to the wall. There was a signal from my legs that a renewed, tremendous effort was called for. I responded and held out with my back against a tree. I looked down at the club which supported me and absorbed the waves of pain from my arm. There was enough light to identify the thing quite distinctly even if I hadn't felt its familiar shape. It was a cricket bat.

It seemed a long walk after that. Certainly it was unsteady, but I kept going and the deadly weapon took pity on me and held me up in the bad moments. I may have passed a person or two, but no one who thought fit, or had the courage, to stop me. The traffic had died down but not the heat and I had the sensation of walking on fire. I was in sight of the flats when I saw people leaving, the remnants of the party perhaps. I held back until they'd gone then let myself into the brightly lit, deserted hall and sat down for a minute on a leather bench beneath a reproduction of Vlaminck's black and snowy waste of a village street with a figure toiling uphill and going no place in particular. After a minute I rang down the lift and made it shakily, but safely, to Julia's door. There was subdued noise within. I opened the door quietly and slipped unseen, I thought, along the hall. I was past the kitchen and the spare room and deciding between bathroom and bedroom when Julia came up behind me with a tread as light as the man in the lane. Yes, it had been a man all right.

Only Julia could have steered me into the bedroom, sat me down on the bed, taken the cricket bat from my hands, and then put it in the wardrobe with the words, 'It isn't cricket.'

Pain plays strange tricks. It can often divert your attention to observe others in a different light. I suddenly caught in Julia's face the conflicting emotions of tenderness, concern, guilt, frustration and bitterness. Conflicting? Well, no. For a moment these expressions lived with equal intensity and harmony in her face.

'Is the party over?' I asked.

'Nearly, but not quite. Go to bed and I'll send them all away.'

I stood up. The head was buzzing now and the arm hurt like hell but I still felt an encouraging response from my legs.

'I need a drink,' I said bravely.

'You need a shower. You're red hot. Where did you fall down, by the way?'

'What do you mean?'

'Hang on.' She went to her dressing table and advanced towards me with a clothes brush. I was covered in dust. She brushed me down with incredible lightness, sensing my pain, but the arm responded.

'Christ almighty!' It was a natural cry.

'Go back to the others,' I said. 'I'll join you in a minute.'

She seemed about to shrug then decided on a nod of compliance. 'As you wish.'

She left me and I went to the bathroom. It was inviting but I resisted the temptation, for the time being, to strip off and let cold water bombard the troubled skin on my arm. I took my time and washed my face and hands and combed my hair. I was sensible enough not to remove my jacket. Any exercise of that kind might make me seize up. Then I had a brief exchange with my face in the mirror and returned to the sitting room. I was just spared Forester. He was saying good-bye and waved to me with an elated, preoccupied air. I seem to recall Roper, Hindmarsh, Kirkstead and (for the first time) the two twelfth men, Lincoln and Coonan. And possibly Ackroyd and Flinders, I couldn't be sure. Thirtle was talking to the everlasting Angie who now had the bitter look of one who has been stranded with the wrong person, while the real prey has escaped. There was no sign of Polly but Julia was talking to Kirkstead and Mrs Gates. She was sipping champagne from one glass and holding another aloft like a trophy. She extended it to me.

'That's whisky,' she said.

Kirkstead was high but not without perception.

'Hello, skipper. You look a bit frayed at the edges,' he said amiably.

'You'll be a bloody sight worse if this game goes the distance,' I replied, yawning to invite distraction.

It worked. He grinned and put his arm round Mrs Gates. 'Home, James,' she said, but they went on to the kitchen together. I went to the chair where Festing had been sitting. I drank the whisky, the pain subsided. Then I went back to the bathroom and was violently sick without too much distress. It was a disciplined performance, as these things go, and soon I felt better. I was glad not to be followed or hovered over. Returning I heard Angie asking Julia if she might stay the night. There was a crisp refusal and suddenly the three of us were alone; Julia, Mrs Gates and myself.

'Where's Polly?' I asked.

'She's gone, disappeared,' said Julia shortly. 'But she might be back, I suppose. Eileen's staying the night. We'll make up a bed on the couch.'

Julia followed my glance at the silent phone. 'We'll switch the phone through to the bedroom, then Eileen won't be disturbed.'

'I shall sleep well tonight,' said Mrs Gates brightly, and she began to clear the debris from the sitting room.

'Well, how was it?' Julia asked.

'Pretty bad, I'd say. How was it *here*, in my absence?'

'Oh, people leaving and talking and a little modest snogging. That sort of thing. I'd say you weren't missed.'

'Did anyone go out for a while, before the phone call, I mean. Any ideas?'

She ran a hand down her leg from knee to ankle.

'Forester perhaps, and maybe Hindmarsh. But I can't be certain. Now what happened to Reg?'

I pulled a face. 'It was no accident. Someone ran him down, then did it all over again. But he's still alive, I think.'

'Were you knocked down?' she asked.

'Yes, but not by a car.'

'Go to the bathroom,' she said. 'God knows, you never seem to be out of the place. I'll get the bed ready. Do you need a hand with anything?'

'No. If the phone rings for me, tell them I'm asleep or something.'

Then I went to the bathroom and took off my clothes.

The cold shower was agonizing bliss. My upper arm was swollen and throbbing, though nothing seemed to be broken. There would be massive bruising by the morning. In the cabinet I found a proprietary brand of painkiller in tablet form. I chewed up four and washed them down with whisky, hoping to strike a reasonable balance between dulling the pain and knocking myself out entirely. I was there quite a time. Once I heard the phone ring and Julia's voice, not shouting, but with a crisp and stubborn note. And it rang again when I was brushing my teeth. Then I couldn't find the bathrobe. Past caring, I wandered nude into Julia's bedroom where she and Eileen Gates were pulling back the sheets.

'There you are,' said Julia. 'Perfect timing. Now get into bed.'

I obeyed and Julia covered me up.

Eileen said good night and Julia turned off the main lights in the bedroom, leaving a soft pink glow from the lamp at her bedside.

'I can't face a bath,' she said. And she kicked off her shoes and pulled off her clothes, leaving them in a heap. She stood there nude with her back to me. Then she bent down and rummaged in a drawer.

'I think I'll wear these,' she said and she slipped on a pair of silk knickers that I had always been fond of. It was a gesture that combined common sense with eroticism. The pain in my arm was converted into the pleasure between my legs.

Julia joined me in bed and came close but avoiding, as if with certain knowledge, the awful arm. She rubbed against my legs, then felt between them with her firm, delicate fingers. Then a little later, with utter lack of selfishness, she practised one of the most intimate acts of love. It was sublime but brief and I wriggled in ecstasy for a short time only. Her lips glistened in the soft light and she kissed me once, very gently. I would like to say that I felt, after that, a sense of finality, a conviction of the end. But that would not be telling the truth. What I can say is that it proved to be the last time we made love together.

'Go to sleep now,' she said. 'You can tell me some more in the morning.'

'I heard the phone ring, twice. Were those calls for me?'

'One was. It was Inspector Green. He wants to see you.'

'I'm surprised he's not beating down the door already.'

'I told him he must wait. He's ringing again at nine. Don't be frightened.'

Frightened? Was I frightened? It sounded so childish. But perhaps that was just the fact of the matter.

'I'll do my best. Just do one thing for me. Ring the hospital and inquire on my behalf after Reg. They'll understand.'

Patiently and quietly Julia carried out my request.

'There is no more news,' she said, putting down the phone. 'His condition is still serious. Ring again at breakfast. And Dr Spilsby sends you his regards.'

When the pain woke me up the bedside light was still on but my watch was missing. I must have left it in the bathroom. I got stiffly but quietly out of bed, trying not to disturb Julia. But she was no longer there. I had that hideous, nightmarish sense of repetition. Julia would be sleepwalking again, hiding behind a door, standing like a statue by a bookcase, or leaning over the balcony. I shuffled into the hall where the light, as before, was burning dimly. I was arrested by the sound of breathing, not from the sitting room where Mrs Gates would be sleeping, but from the open door of Polly's room. I gritted my teeth (how full of meaning is that phrase at certain times) and stepped into the room. The cover was thrown off and piled at the foot of the made-up, unslept-in bed. Someone was lying on it, fast asleep. No sooner had I reasoned that Polly had returned, slipping in quietly in the dark, than I realized the truth. Julia, still in her splendid knickers, was sprawled on the bed clutching a pillow, like a doll or a teddy-bear, to her breasts. She had been waiting for her lover to come home and had fallen asleep.

I went to the bathroom, found my watch and grabbed the painkillers. Lurching like an old ruin into the kitchen I found the whisky, poured a great slug and added water. Then, recklessly, down with the pills again. I went back to bed and tried to think things out but mercifully this futile exercise succeeded only in sending me to sleep again. But the night had still not dispensed its full erotic content. I dreamed of the two nude girls rising up at the foot of the bed, pointing at me, convulsed with noiseless laughter as Fitzgerald, back from the dead, also nude with his penis thrust out, emerged from the wardrobe and came up behind them. And worst of all, completing this gallery of nudes, my wife Peggy was sitting by my side with her legs wide apart and a strange twisted smile on her face. Then the sound I had heard in the lane, a beating of wings that grew louder and louder, a hideous din in my ears ending with a clap like thunder as the horrible images disintegrated.

When I awoke it was daylight and Julia was in the room, moving very quietly and getting dressed. At last my eyes stayed open and I shifted restlessly.

'What time is it?' I asked.

Julia scowled. She looked pale and tense. 'About half-past eight. How are you feeling?'

'I'm not sure yet. Pretty awful, I should think.'

'Stay put. Eileen's making coffee.' And she gathered up the dirty clothes and went to dump them in the linen basket. Wearily I turned to the demanding agent, the instrument of torture, the telephone. I rang Peggy, hoping she would allow me that crucial space of time when you can get your word in first. But at once she said, 'I suppose you're ringing at this hour to say that you're not coming home to lunch?'

'Now hold on, Peggy, hold on. Please don't hang up.'

She said nothing.

I told her all I knew about Festing but made no reference to my own experience.

'I'm sorry, Jack,' she said gently, 'I'm very sorry. Don't worry. I'll explain it to the girls.'

'I will ring,' I said in quiet desperation, 'I will ring as soon as I can and tell you when I'm coming home. Is Hester still there?'

'Yes, she's here. We're all very well. Are *you* all right?'

'Of course.'

Her response was a laugh that might have just passed for one of Julia's – a blend of scorn, exasperation and affection.

'Well, good-bye then. We are going to nine o'clock mass.'

I rang Willie. He had heard the news about Festing. I told him about my visit, summons rather, to the hospital and the conversation with Spilsby. The rest I kept quiet about. Willie sensed, quite rightly, that Spilsby was a lead to follow up.

'He's interesting in himself,' I said, 'but I doubt if he'll say much to the Press. It's just a hunch and I could be wrong. But don't send Smith.'

Willie swore fluently. 'I must confess that this is getting rather out of hand, old son.'

I felt rather like confessing myself but replied, 'Well, what do you want me to do?'

'Don't be daft. It stands out a mile. We must have your story of what happened last night.'

I hedged. 'I'm not at all sure if I can do that sort of thing to your satisfaction, let alone mine.'

'Stop quibbling,' said Willie. 'Just sit down, write it out and phone it in. I'm going in now. We expect to hear from you by lunchtime at the latest.'

'What about the cricket, though?'

'We'll want that as well, dammit. Stop feeling sorry for yourself – and the others – and start grafting. This is a newspaper. We do have readers, you know. And I have an editor who is painfully aware of competition. Do you want me to lose my job?'

I waited and then fed him a bit more.

'I think the police may want to see me, quite soon.'

'Couldn't be better. Stop backing into the limelight. Just rush into it and then we'll all be happy.'

This was too much, even from Willie. 'I'll do my best,' I said defiantly.

Willie was adamant. He sensed my reluctance and acknowledged the special pressures that were being applied to me in this affair. He responded with a final barrage of encouragement and exhortation and then, sensibly, rang off.

I rang Brooke-Stanley. There was no reply. Curious.

I rang (a sub-conscious touch here) Forester. There was no reply. I rang Abbott. There again was no reply because he was engaged. I had an instinct that this particular phone had been taken off the hook. I rang Hunt at his hotel and got a dusty answer from reception. He just wasn't available.

I was thinking of another ploy when Inspector Green rang me.

'What can I do for you, Mr Green?'

It was a silly way to begin but then we had started badly in the first place with Festing's needlessly mysterious and irritating manoeuvres that night at the Rossetti. And it was silly to let Green get on my nerves but the renaissance of the pain in my arm suggested that he had done just that.

'I really must ask you to see me as soon as possible, Mr Stenton. This morning, perhaps?'

'Why the rush?'

A note of patience had crept into Green's voice. I should have realized that this was a sign of determination.

'Mr Stenton, there are two very grave matters where we think you may be of considerable help to the police. One, as you know, is murder, and the other is probably attempted murder. Now I don't want to go into details, certainly not on the phone, but I'm sure you must agree that it's reasonable – especially in view of what's happened to Mr Festing – that we should meet on a friendly, informal basis. The alternative, though inevitable, would be tiresome and time-wasting. Surely you accept this?'

'Yes, I'm afraid I do. But I'm a working journalist, you know. And I have a very tough assignment today.'

I heard Green sigh. And then he went on in the same level tone. 'And I am a working policeman,' he said. 'Do you want me to come to you in Abbey Road, or meet me here at the police station, or anywhere you choose?'

'I'd prefer the police station.'

'When, then?'

'It must be after lunch. Will, say, three o'clock do?'

'Yes. You know the way?'

'No trouble. You can count on me.'

'I'm sure of that. By the way, Mr Stenton, are you feeling any better this morning?'

'Any better than when?'

'The early hours of this morning when you were reported seen in the Abbey Road, walking unsteadily and carrying, it is thought, a cricket bat.'

'I'll see you later, Mr Green,' I said and put the phone down.

I shouted for Julia and Mrs Gates appeared.

'Julia's gone out. She'll be back soon. If you want to get up you'll find clean clothes in the bathroom. If you don't, stay where you are and I'll bring you breakfast in bed.'

'I'll get up, thank you.'

Mrs Gates hovered for a moment, slightly out of character.

'Did you sleep well?' I asked.

'That couch is more comfortable than my bed at home.'

Mrs Gates looked trim and smart as always but a little exhausted. But her eyes were shining brightly. Perhaps Kirkstead had nipped back for a nightcap.

'Did Polly turn up eventually?'

'There's been no sign of her,' said Mrs Gates. And she left the room.

I got out of bed. I was stiff as a board and I ached all over. I made a tentative thrust with the arm and yelped with pain. I thought it might simply come away, at any time, in protest from the rest of my body. The arm was swollen, both numb and painful at the same time, and badly bruised. I found another huge bruise on the inside of my right wrist that could be seen. There were abrasions on both knees and another small bruise high on my left temple. This was a tender spot and very painful to the touch. My face looked yellow and rather unpleasant and my hair needed washing. I could have been worse. I was not entirely deficient in will power and so I summoned up some reserves and got down to getting ready for the day. I presented myself forty minutes later, a record slow time for me, but I looked clean and fresh and quite presentable in my white shirt, maroon lightweight jacket and grey worsted slacks.

The living room was spotless again and so was the kitchen. It was ten o'clock and Mrs Gates was just leaving. Julia was back.

'Thank you, Eileen dear,' said Julia, who was hard at it with the Russians again, 'I'll see you on Wednesday.'

'Ring me if you want me,' said Mrs Gates and she went.

I sat down stiffly and looked at Julia. She was wearing a dark brown dress with shoes of even darker brown and dark green stockings that appeared to be made of real silk. Her nails and face were beautifully painted and her hair was any old how. She certainly knew how to dress. I grinned, then started laughing.

'What's so funny?'

'You are sometimes. Now, I don't want any breakfast but I'd like some coffee with whisky in it.'

'Yes, master.' With a mocking smile she went to do my bidding.

Returning, she poured coffee and put down a whisky bottle by the cup. I helped myself and swallowed two more painkillers.

'Do you want me to look at your arm?' she asked.

'No, thank you.'

'What about your wrist and your head?'

'They're doing fine. Observant little thing, aren't you?'

Julia poured coffee for herself and put some whisky in it.

'Perhaps we'd better stick to the hard stuff today,' she said, and leaned back in her chair looking like Calamity Jane.

'I've forgotten about Reg!' I shouted in real dismay. 'Phone, phone!'

'I rang early this morning, just before breakfast. He's still on the danger list. Keep in touch. That's all.'

'I'll go round later.'

'It was that Dr Spilsby again. He sounds rather flirtatious.'
She put a hand to her head. 'My hair's in a dreadful mess.'

There was a familiar glint of lust in the dark green eyes.
Then she stood up and said, 'I'll get the cricket bat.'

I examined the bat very closely. It was new and still had
to make contact with a cricket ball, though certainly one
edge was bruised. Need I say more. I placed it on the couch.
It lay between us like a sword, a beautiful object and a
deadly weapon.

'I can't be absolutely certain,' I said, 'but it probably be-
longs to one of the Australians. Quite a few of them are
using this make on the tour.'

'I suppose,' said Julia, picking it up deliberately, 'we
should keep our hands off it . . . it may be needed as evidence.' Then she held it up with ease. 'I must say it is a most
appropriate weapon to clobber *you* with. Are you quite sure
it was a man?'

'Yes, I am.'

'Why?'

'I just know, that's all,' I snapped.

She shrugged her shoulders and put the bat down.

'Green rang,' I said, 'I'm seeing him at the police station
at three. What are you doing for lunch?'

'I'm out to lunch. Stay here and help yourself. But what
about the homestead?'

'I've explained the situation to Peggy.'

'Will you be staying the night?'

There was something about the way she put this question
that made me feel she would prefer me out of the way.

'Don't worry, I shall certainly be going home tonight.'

'Who's worrying?' She frowned.

I stood up with a cheerful groan, picked up the cricket bat
and placed it by a bookcase in the corner of the room.
Another matter came to mind.

'Sorry to go on about it, but Green is bound to find out
about Polly and Fitzgerald. Have you the slightest idea where
she is?'

'Yes, I do have a slight idea.'

There was an awkward silence. Julia looked bored and restless.

'How much are you involved, Julia?'

Her reply to this was simply, 'We are all involved. Now have another drink and put your feet up. I'll see you later, perhaps.' She kissed me gently on the cheek and left. The Sunday papers, untouched and unloved, were to hand. I had a strong desire to let them be, but remembering Festing I picked up his newspaper. His copy was on the front page with a turn to the back.

Under the headline 'These Men are Dangerous' were seven mug shots of fast bowlers, three Australians, two Englishmen and two West Indians. There was a lively knockabout intro, certainly the work of a keen and diligent sub, followed by Festing's own call to arms in the matter of the current rash of very fast, hostile and intimidating bowling that was bringing the game into disrepute and ruining it entirely as a contest of grace, skill and stamina. There was a scornful dismissal of a call for protective headgear, it being Festing's contention that the present laws of the game, if fairly but strenuously applied, could stop the rot. As might be expected, Festing's prejudiced and crusading spirit set the tone of the piece, though he was sensible enough to observe that the absence of very fast bowling would take the zest out of the game and keep the crowds away. Together with this were some pungent if rather cryptic remarks on certain leading batsmen (not named) who just lived in hope that one day soon the vintage crop of fast men would become exhausted; and then some observations on other batsmen, who with a blend of natural ability, sound technique and moral fibre were acquitting themselves with some distinction. I noticed that he also had the nous to mention the in-between category: those who were George medallists one day and palpable funks the next. But allowing for historical perspective and balance, it was undeniable, Festing contended, that even the best of the batsmen were now subjected to very special strains and tensions unknown to their predecessors. At this stage my potent whisky-coffee and painkillers took over and I dozed off.

The ringing in my ears seemed to last for centuries, rather like those endless panoramas described by de Quincey, the opium eater. It was the phone and I struggled out of sleep (for once) to answer it. It was Brooke-Stanley.

'Jack? Jack, is that you?'

'Yes, I think so.'

'Are you in bed?'

'No, no. Just dozing. I had a bad night.'

'Never mind that,' said the President brusquely. 'Can you come round?'

'Yes, I suppose so. Are you at home?'

'Where else? I'm on my own. It's Francis's day off.'

The President sounded excited and vigorous.

'I've worked it out, my boy, I think I've worked it out.'

'What? You've heard about Festing then?'

'Yes, yes. It all fits into place now.'

'Why don't you call the police?' My reluctance to play detective was becoming ever stronger in these increasingly sinister circumstances. Too many people were playing games.

But all this drew from the President was the unexpected, 'Are you lunching with Julia?'

'No, she's gone out.'

'Then come round here. What better?'

I should have refused on the spot but said, 'I've some writing to do and, for your information, I have an appointment with our friend Green at three.'

'All the better. We can have a little lunch before you go. Let's say a quarter to two.'

Anticipating a further protest, but confident in his will-power he rang off. Oddly enough, this exchange transformed my lethargy into action. I took some foolscap sheets from the bureau and wrote, without too much trouble, a laconic account of my visit to the hospital. It stopped short at the time of my leaving there, and my unhappy stroll down the lane. Surely that was the best bit, though? And here I was leaving it out. But enough was enough. Then like a robot I began to write about the cricket ... this didn't go at all well. Even the act of pouring another whisky was enough to put me off drinking it. I dithered and waffled and paced about the room. My dilemma was resolved when I looked at my watch. It was two o'clock. I left everything and walked, none too briskly, to the President's house in Elm Tree Road.

The sun was out now but the heat unmitigated. The streets were dead and even the traffic seemed asleep. I walked on, the perfect fool and an ideal audience for the President's amateur theatricals.

The front door was open as usual. I went in and called out. There was no response. I went into the sitting room, then the dining room where the table was laid (a little carelessly) for two. I called again. No one answered and I thought the President might be in his study on the first floor. Back in the hall I was about to climb the stairs when I heard a noise. I looked round and found the source.

At the end of the hall the door leading to the wine cellar stood open and even in the still air it had managed some movement and was creaking very slightly on its hinges. Another open door. I felt uneasy. By my side in a superbly carved wooden cylinder was the President's collection of walking sticks. There was one very heavy, uncouth-looking piece that looked as if it had been hacked from some iron-hard African tree and then given a perfunctory polish. I took it and advanced to the head of the stairs leading down to the cellar. I called loudly for the last time. Dead silence. And then, and then, I heard another noise, a barely perceptible trickling sound that would have been smothered by a footfall, a passing car, or even a call to lunch from a distant garden. I walked slowly down the stairs.

The cellar floor was awash with red wine and red blood.

The President was on his side with one eye, wide open and in the early stages of death, glaring at me with the final accusation. It seemed to be saying, 'Why didn't you come sooner? Now it's too late.' The back of his head was broken and the thin grey hair had already turned red. A section of the wine racks that held the President's precious clarets had been torn down and were scattered on and around him. Most of them had broken, but not long ago. The liquid was still draining quietly away. I stood on the bottom step, leaning on the stick rather as I had done on the cricket bat earlier this same morning. It was a dreadful sight but strangely enough quite bearable. The worst thing was the dread, the despair, the utter desolation of spirit that invaded my being. Who was it, what was it, and where was it all going to end? Another man might have sensed evil. I could only manage a feeling of profound disgust at the human condition.

I stood there wondering what to do when I heard a firm step in the hall above. I moved upstairs with astonishing speed and stealth but spoilt it all when I slammed my arm against the wall and swore loudly. Two men were blocking the hall. They both wore blue suits and one of them was Mr Green.

'Mr Stenton,' he said chidingly, 'what on earth are you doing now?'

Suddenly I felt my knees going (at last!) and the men came forward and relieved me of the stick. The younger man guided me to a chair in the sitting room and stood by me while Green went down to the cellar. He was soon back and located the phone by the fireplace. He looked grave, but amazingly produced a sympathetic smile.

'Now just you take it easy, Mr Stenton. This is not one of your good days.'

As he began speaking rapidly into the phone, the President's beautiful clock began to chime. It was 2.15.

I was just on time for my appointment at three with Inspector Green, though this was probably due to the fact that I was driven there with him from Elm Tree Road just a few minutes before the hour. I spent three hours or more at the police station. There was food and drink (including the hard stuff which Inspector Green, like Dr Spilsby, kept in his filing cabinet), and long sustained spells of interrogation in an atmosphere of consideration and courtesy.

To begin with, I told Green that there was unfinished and urgently needed copy lying in Julia's flat and that my newspaper would not be best pleased if they did not hear from me. Green said that although it appeared there were no witnesses to the crime in Elm Tree Road, the presence of neighbours, passers-by and then the arrival of police cars and an ambulance had made it inevitable that reporters from press, radio and television were already on the scene, and that in view of the latest development in my situation it was imperative that I spoke to no one and that my newspaper would just have to do without my work. He suggested that this decision would prove, for me, more of a relief than a burden and I was forced to agree with him. Green agreed to ring both my Editor and Sports Editor and left me alone for a while, though I noticed a policeman standing just outside the door.

When he returned I thought I would get in first and asked, 'Tell me, Mr Green, why you happened to turn up when I was down in the cellar?'

'Ah yes. Well, you know, we've been keeping an eye on your movements after last night's little episode. I was informed as soon as you left the flat in the Abbey Road this afternoon. So I took my sergeant for a little walk, to keep you company, as it were. We heard you calling from just inside the house and then, you might say, we got the wind up and followed you in. It's as simple as that.'

'I doubt if the rest of it will be,' I said sullenly.

'Well, that to some extent will depend on you, I'm sure. Now try to relax and drink some more of that whisky. You're beginning to look better already.'

I couldn't answer for my looks but I knew that I felt

lousy. And the whisky failed to obliterate the taste of dust and ashes in my mouth.

'Are all police stations as stuffy as this one?' I asked, taking off my jacket.

Green took off his coat too and turned to tug at the window. Apart from a slight ripple of flesh above the belt he looked very fit and hard. When he turned round I saw that his sandy hair, though fine, was still copious and that he was given to freckles. 'Now let's get on with it,' he said.

'To be quite frank, Mr Stenton, I not only find this case confusing but I must admit to you that my experience of investigating murder cannot possibly match that of yours at cricket. In truth I've only just made up my mind about the line of questioning. I have decided to begin at the beginning.'

He spread his hands on the desk and began.

'Do you know who killed Fitzgerald?'

'No. Come to that I didn't know he was murdered "officially".'

'Do you know who tried to kill Reginald Festing?'

'No.'

'Do you know – and here I'm in the dark as I'm sure you were – who made a violent assault on you early this morning?'

'No. But you're right, someone did.'

'Do you know who killed Mr Brooke-Stanley?'

'No.'

'Have you the slightest, even quite groundless, suspicion, of any person or persons who may have committed these crimes?'

'No, not really.'

'This stonewalling isn't very productive, Mr Stenton. You never played your cricket in this fashion.'

'Oh it has been known. I once took three hours to score 26.'

'Good gracious. Where was that?'

'At Headingley. They usually appreciate that sort of thing

up there, but on this occasion, being a southerner, they rubbished me.'

For a moment Green looked like a non-smoker who was dying for a fag. But he took a sip of whisky and said, 'May we talk about Festing for a moment?'

'By all means. What's the latest on him, by the way?'

'Not so good. There is very severe brain damage. If he recovers he may never say anything sensible again.'

That was bad enough but it didn't encourage me to expand. I dug my heels in.

'May I remind you, Mr Green, that it was through Festing that I met *you*. Perhaps you can tell *me* something for a change?'

'It's better if I ask the questions,' he said coolly, in spite of the sweat on his brow. 'Did Festing tell you anything at all concerning the death of Fitzgerald?'

'Not really. Have you read his piece today?'

'Yes.'

'Well, it's all there. A considered account of his views on the fast-bowling business. He repeated it all again at the party, but in a much more intemperate fashion. He was a little drunk.'

'Did he ever mention Fitzgerald's relations with other people, other cricketers, perhaps?'

This was a sly thrust and I countered with the truth as far as I knew it.

'Yes. There was a hint that Hunt, for entirely personal reasons, was not too fond of Fitzgerald.'

For a second Green averted his eyes and I was sure he knew this story already. 'Now I'll be honest with you,' he said. And I believed him on the spot.

The car that knocked down Festing belonged to Hunt, or rather a good friend had lent it to him for the duration of the tour. It is a blue Jaguar saloon and Hunt parked it in a side street near Julia French's flat before last night's party. When he left the party just after 11.30, it was missing. The person who stole it – supposing that Hunt's story is true –

tried to kill Festing and then left it, a master stroke, you might say, in the lane behind the hospital. We discovered it at early light this morning. Mr Hunt has confirmed that this was his car. He says he might have got round to reporting the theft when he'd recovered from his night out. Apparently he had other things on his mind that took priority.'

'Women perhaps?'

Green attempted an expression of mock horror that didn't quite come off and said, 'But there's another thing. When we put it to him, Mr Hunt confirmed that there was a brand-new cricket bat on the back seat. What about that, Mr Stenton?'

What about it indeed. Green had me there and I told him the story of the attack in the lane. His eyes travelled from the bruise on my wrist to the bruise on my temple.

'And your left arm seems to be giving you trouble,' he said.

'That's for sure.' And I drank some more of his whisky.

'You're a fool, Mr Stenton, and an irresponsible one at that. You have left your own life in danger and might in some degree be considered responsible for the murder of Mr Brooke-Stanley. You should have called the police immediately. You might have saved us a lot of trouble, oh a great deal of trouble. Now there may be no end to it.' And he shook his head in dismay and disbelief.

His rebuke, though justified, did not bring out the best in me. I looked at my watch and said, 'How much longer is this going on?'

He treated this with affectionate contempt and said, 'Now tell me, please, about your talks with Mr Brooke-Stanley.'

I gave him the edited version. That the President in his way was just as secretive and given to obscure hints as Festing had been, though perhaps more mischievous and certainly more autocratic. Wilfully and foolishly I suppressed the facts about the President's talk with Fitzgerald at Nottingham and his mention of the postcards. Green certainly wasn't onto this and his next question came as no surprise.

'Why then did you go to see Brooke-Stanley this afternoon?'

'He rang me at Miss French's flat where I was writing my copy and asked me to lunch.'

'Is that all?'

'No.' And I gave him a little more of the truth. 'He sounded agitated and very keen to tell me something. Indeed he said something like "I've worked it out, my boy" and that was when I told him he should go to the police. I hope you can swallow that,' I added savagely.

'Oh I can, Mr Stenton, alas I can, only too well.'

There was a knock at the door and a constable came in with tea and sandwiches. Green smiled encouragingly.

'Thank you, but I'm not hungry and I don't want tea.

'That tea is coffee,' said Green mournfully. 'Why don't you ring your wife? Or anyone you choose. We shall be through within half an hour at the most. Please excuse me, I'll be back shortly.'

Green left the room, taking his coffee with him. I lifted the phone. There was no dialling tone but presently a woman (police switchboard, no doubt) asked me what I wanted and I gave my home number.

Peggy answered and said, 'Oh God, Jack, I can't bear it.'

'Can't bear what?' I replied, not sure what she was getting at.

'There's been a news flash – about a murder in St John's Wood. They say it's Philip.'

'They say right,' I said grimly. Then, adopting police jargon, 'Myself, though not guilty, of course, am at present helping the police with their inquiries. But this is to say that I'll be home before long, and that's a promise. Try to get the children to bed early. I must go now.'

It seemed sensible to cut Peggy short, and anyway that had always been my style on the phone. Then I rang Julia. There was no reply. Were the police listening in? Green came back and said 'I gather that a Miss Parsons is at present staying at Miss French's flat, where indeed you have been staying for the last few days?'

'That's right.'

Green looked at a notebook he had brought back with him.

'But according to a Mrs Gates, Miss Parsons wasn't there last night. Not all night, anyway.'

'That's probably right, too. Why don't you ask Miss French?'

'We've tried. But she's not at home.'

'Well, she was this morning.'

'Do you know where she's gone?'

'No idea.'

'Do you know where Miss Parsons is?'

'Haven't the faintest.'

Green opened out a little. 'We have established – and it seems to be common knowledge in certain circles – that during the first Test Match at Nottingham, Miss Parsons spent two nights with Fitzgerald at a hotel in the town.'

'That's possible.'

Green had a fit of shrewdness or sympathy, possibly both. 'That's enough for now. We haven't got very far, I would say, but I think you've had enough for the day. You may remember some more after a good night's rest.'

'Let's settle for the rest first,' I said and stood up. I felt tired and creaky.

'You need a day or two in bed,' said Green in a fatherly fashion. 'At least that would keep you out of mischief.'

'Oh, I don't know. You can do a lot of harm in bed. Now when do you want to see me again?'

'Perhaps sometime tomorrow – if you're up to it. I don't want to pin you down. And then there's the cricket, of course. Might they abandon the game?'

'They might. Who knows, it might be the only way to stop the murders.'

'Now that's very interesting,' said Green. 'Why do you say that?'

'Just an instinct.'

'I like your instincts, Mr Stenton. I like them very much.'

Green insisted on driving me home to Hampstead. He drove with competence and sureness of direction like a blessedly silent taxi driver. He merely said, 'Good-bye and thank you,' and then drove off leaving me by the gate. I turned round as the front door opened. It was Peggy. She was looking fresh and attractive and anxious. She smiled warmly but her eyes were looking me up and down and responding with a troubled light. She began to open her arms then changed her mind and stood aside as I entered my own home.

'The children are in bed,' Peggy whispered, 'but certainly not asleep. Hester's upstairs with them.'

I stood in the hall, feeling bewildered and trapped. For one moment I was terrified of being in my own home again.

Peggy took firm action. 'Now then, talking can wait. If you want to tell me anything at all, tell me in your own good time. So why don't you go to bed and I'll bring you anything you need.'

'No, not bed. Not just yet. I think I'll sit in the study for a bit. And though I seem to have been sipping whisky all day, I could do with another one right now.'

As I turned to go upstairs I realized that at least I might have given her a kiss. Turning to do so, I encountered her with the same idea in mind. In the event we merely knocked our heads together. But we both laughed, that was something.

The study was an L-shaped room overlooking the heath. There were some books, a table and two battered armchairs. I sat down and for a moment listened to the typical heath noises that came in through the open window; dogs, children, shouting adolescents and traffic grinding up the hill. I was back home in the bosom of my family. Peggy came in with a tray carrying whisky, water and a heavy glass tumbler. She put the tray on the table, poured out whisky, added water and brought the glass to my chair. Peggy was an ash blonde and a big, handsome lass. She had a generous mouth and a husky voice without a trace of affectation. She was – or rather had been till of late – a warm, good-natured woman and, dare I say it, full of fun with a love of horseplay and practical jokes. She was an accomplished but dangerous tennis player, a powerful swimmer and a very good hurdler in her day. She could have broken Julia in half.

'Do you want anything to eat?' she asked.

'No thanks. If you don't mind I'll stay here for a while. And if Hester's staying the night, I'll take the bed in the attic.'

'She is staying the night and you'll be sleeping with me in our room. I've put your things out. Go to bed when you feel like it. I shan't be late up.'

Peggy went downstairs. I sipped the whisky but seemed to have lost the painkillers en route. No matter. I was getting used to my aches and pains. There was a phone extension on the desk and I rang Julia. This time she answered. She sounded calm and steady like a mother waiting patiently to speak. Once again like a man condemned to perpetually breaking stones in the stifling air of a quarry, I laboured away at the facts and the day's events since I had last seen her. She was not entirely uninformed. She had spoken with Inspector Green but only on the phone. A policeman had called round and taken away the cricket bat.

'Did he ask about Polly?' I inquired.

'Yes.'

'Is she back with you?'

'No.'

'Did you go out to look for her?'

'Yes.'

'Did you find her?'

'Yes. She was in bed with somebody, the silly bitch.'

'Does Green know about this?'

'No.'

'You may have to tell him in the end.'

'I don't see why. I should be careful what you say, if I

were you. What with Festing and now poor old Philip, you seem to be in dead trouble, if you'll pardon the phrase.'

'Perhaps Mrs Gates should spend the night with you?' I suggested.

'I can't think why. I enjoy being on my own,' she said perversely.

'What are your plans for tomorrow?'

'I shall go to the cricket,' she said, 'if they don't stop the match. What about you? Has Peggy put you to bed?'

'Not quite. I'm alone in the study trying to think things out.'

'Don't strain yourself,' she said with her nervous laugh breaking out.

'When and where shall we meet?'

'Oh, I'll be around. You're sure to find me. If I'm missing I'll leave a note in the flat.'

'Right then. Any calls for me?'

'Abbott rang. I told him you were at home. Good-bye.'

It was hot and getting dark but a slight breeze blew in from the heath. I tried to think things out and to establish, however sketchily, the order of events since Thursday morning. I tried to get straight my position and responsibilities in this affair which seemed to be burning unchecked with steady but savage intensity like a forest fire. But I was too tired. The people and the places would not form any logical pattern, the days seemed to stick together, refusing to be separated. My mind abdicated and slipped back into the past.

I found myself reflecting on the blessings and curses of the natural aptitudes, those which bestow an innate athleticism, a ball sense, that seemingly effortless power that denotes perfect timing, that physical co-ordination which is quite instinctive and, though cultivated, can never be taught. It is said that natural athletes have it all their own way. Perhaps they do for a time. Where cricket was concerned I swept through school and university and then into county and Test cricket, playing very much in the 'natural' and 'attractive' style that catches the eye and brings in the crowds and, to be fair, often wins matches for the side. I was well into my Test career before that innate aptitude, the gift from the gods, deserted me for ever. It was in a Test Match against Australia at Old Trafford. I was at the wicket for two days, a deadly grind, attempting scoring strokes only when they seemed as secure and assured as a bank manager's income. I scored 178 not out. They were painful runs and though they helped materially to save the day I scarcely enjoyed making even one of them. It was the end of my 'golden age'. There were many more runs and occasional triumphs in store. There was no collapse, only a small nervous breakdown, you might say, but my batting and my cricket were never quite the same again. I began to think when I should have been feeling, and to feel when I should have been thinking.

Now I was at sea in the roaring forties; a journalist though by no means a 'natural'; a bit of an expert, a gambler in fits and starts, a playboy on a modest scale, and a proud father who, though straying from time to time, had only recently revealed a destructive attitude towards himself and his marriage. And now the Lord's Murders (that's for sure what the label would be in tomorrow's papers) had seized me like a man who wanders heedlessly in a very dangerous zone, and put me to the torture. I could think of war and famine and the intolerable personal suffering of millions. I could think of the music of Mozart and the plays of Shakespeare. But all these things, whether for good or bad, did nothing to mitigate my own feelings of frustration, grievance and, I suppose, guilt. The passion for Julia was hopeless for me and for her and all those who came into contact with us. Could it be snapped decisively like a stick, or would it have to wither – or rot away like a leaf fallen from a tree?

Peggy in her nightgown roused me at eleven. Unthinking, I stripped off in the bedroom and reached for my pyjamas. There was a gasp and I turned to face Peggy.

'Good God, Jack. What is happening to you?' she said,

staring at the great purple blotches that were blooming on my arm.

'Someone tried to kill me.'

'Who? Who?'

'A man with a cricket bat.'

There followed the inevitable discussion of doctors, treatment, X-rays and so on but I was irritable and adamant and Peggy controlled her agitation very well. I yielded only to a little simple and soothing first aid, then we went to bed. There were no gentle advances, no affectionate touches, no songs without words. Indeed, there were very few words. I sensed Peggy wide awake in the dark on the other side of the bed. If there was a restlessness and tension she kept quiet and still about it. The dark masses of furniture in the room assumed their familiar night-time shapes and attitudes. The ceiling resisted for a time, sliding and curving like a gentle ocean swell. But I stared it out and at last it was still. Before I drifted into sleep the church clock on the hill did its work on behalf of time. The chimes of midnight sounded harsh and reluctant. But it was the end of another day.

Monday

I had another bad dream that night. It was long and ludicrous, repetitive and frightening and, I suppose, a classic of
its kind. I was back in my twenties and batting again. There
was an enormous crowd but it seemed miles away, inces-
santly murmuring, then crashing in my ears with great force
like the sea against the rocks. The game was being played in
pitch darkness. There were fielders all around me whispering
and jeering but I couldn't see them. Nor could I see the man
who was bowling to me. All I ever saw, and that at the last
moment, was the ball, a terrible projectile coming at me
again and again, whistling and screaming past my head and
body. I never made any contact at all, and this was the real
nightmarish horror of the thing. They couldn't get me out
and I seemed doomed to stay there for ever, a figure of fun in
an awful state of dread. I was there for centuries without
ever making a run. At last the ball of ultimate destruction
burst through the darkness, exploded on my head, killed me,
and then woke me up. I seemed to recall sweating and moaning and Peggy's quiet voice coaxing me to sleep again. Peace
followed and the next thing I knew was the early morning
light and Peggy, made-up and dressed and standing by the
bed with a cup of coffee.

'It's a quarter to seven,' she said. 'And I know that if
you're determined to go through with it today you'll want
an early start.'

I sat up and groaned.

'How's the arm?'

'Bearable, I hope. And you're right. There's a lot to be
done before the cricket. Any phone calls yet?'

'There may have been, but I took the phone off the hook. I'll put it back in a few minutes. Seven is quite early enough for phone calls.'

I took the coffee and drank it. It was strong and luke-warm, just how I like it.

'Did I have a nightmare, by the way?'

'Yes, you did. It sounded pretty bad.'

'Sounded? What did I say?'

'Not much that made sense. You kept wanting to hit somebody. Me perhaps?'

'No. It was a thing rather than a person. The cricket ball, in fact.'

Peggy took the cup from my hand. 'Your bath will be ready in ten minutes. Don't go to sleep again unless you discover that you just can't get out of bed. That would be the best thing – but there's little hope, I suppose?'

'Not a chance. Why don't you leave me alone and get some breakfast. I'm hungry.'

I waited five minutes or so then got out of bed. It was an awkward performance, painful to experience and no doubt painful to behold. The arm was throbbing cheerfully, like an engine in an ageing ship. I accepted it as the motive power that would get me through the day. For a while I looked out into the deserted heath which was waiting to accept the heat of the day. In the bathroom the water was running and Peggy was waiting for me. Very gently she took off my pyjamas, said, 'The water should be about right,' and steered me into the bath. She brought a shaving mirror and tackle and said, 'You'd better shave in the bath, if you can manage it.'

I did manage it. Then Peggy steadied me as I lurched from the water, dried me in spite of my protests, and looked on in a state of resigned frustration as I proceeded to dress myself with infinite clumsiness. I put on the lightweight suit with the light blue tie to match, the white cotton and superbly ironed shirt, and finally, bending down and cursing, the dark-blue suede shoes.

'There. That's not too bad,' I said, sweating heavily.

'I've seen worse,' she replied. 'You could do with a haircut. Now come down to breakfast.'

Peggy had arranged matters well. The children and Hester were still in bed, maybe under orders, and Peggy and I breakfasted alone in the dining room. It was a thoughtful, formal touch. I had expected the kitchen. I felt like a child returning to school after the holidays. I lived up to my threat of a good appetite and enjoyed a hearty breakfast. Shades of the condemned man? Then Peggy looked at me thoughtfully and said, 'What can I do to help you today?'

I had a touch of panic. 'I'm not sure.'

'I'm entirely at your disposal.'

There was a very long pause threatened by an imminent fit of bad temper and rejection on my part. Then I began to talk at random. She listened with great composure but her breathing quickened and she clenched one hand very tightly around a table fork.

I talked on. It was a fluent performance, packed with the selected facts, and as much sincerity as I could muster. It was the best I could do and the most I was capable of at that time. I told Peggy more about Julia than I had ever done before but there seemed no point in trying to accommodate the morbid, erotic elements that had played such an important part in our relationship. It's possible that they may have been the very things that would have interested Peggy most. Indeed, I know that there are some women to whom you can say anything, but anything. Their eyes may narrow and their voices become very quiet, but by word and gesture they will urge you to go on. But you can go too far, and I didn't tell Peggy the whole truth about the love and games of myself and Julia, or even hint at the possibility of two lesbians at large into the bargain. I told myself that these matters were not entirely relevant to the matter in hand.

I went on to tell Peggy about the party and what happened to Festing and after that what happened to me. I told

128

her about my discovery of Brooke-Stanley's body and my conversations with the police. As with Green, I suppressed the story of the postcards and, by doing so, inevitably separated my affair with Julia from the murders, the attempted murders and, it could be, I reflected, the murders still to come. To this day I can't explain why but the fact was that in one or two vital matters I was utterly secretive to the point of dishonesty. As in the case of Festing, or Brooke-Stanley perhaps, it may have been vanity, sheer foolishness, a natural subterfuge, or a simple inability to comprehend the scope and seriousness of the issues involved. But soon I began to stumble, repeat myself, raise my voice as if to protest my innocence, then finally ground to a halt. It must have appeared like an appeal for help from a guilty man.

Peggy was sensible, sensitive, but pertinent.

'I see. Or do I? There must be more to it than that.'

'Of course there is.'

It occurred to me that I was lying and telling the truth at the same time.

'It's not so much concealing things, you know, rather a problem of fitting the pieces together in any form that makes sense. Oh dear.' And the words began to let me down again.

Peggy raised both hands, palms outward, and pushed them gently towards me. It was the fending off, the affectionate protest, the considerate rejection of further explanations and apologies.

'That will do. Now, at least, there is something very terrible to worry about.'

I laughed and wished I hadn't. There was a most painful, reciprocal spasm from my arm.

Peggy stood up.

'Do go and see the children, Jack. No need to make a fuss. They know there's something very difficult and complicated going on. Just see them and give them a hug – even if it's with one arm only. I'll rescue you in ten minutes. Then we can go to the study while they have breakfast with Hester.'

'That reminds me. I haven't seen Hester yet.'

'Hester can wait. You know that and so does she. She is like a battleship at anchor, God bless her. And sometimes I think she's fonder of you than I am.' Peggy gave me one of her tough, affectionate looks and left the room. I knew there was something she had left unsaid.

Upstairs I heard the noise of children climbing out of bed, their voices high-pitched and bickering and ready for the fray. And with total recall there rang again in my ears the cry of a child years ago at Tunbridge Wells, that pierced my concentration and got me out for 5 when I was in the mood for getting 500.

Afterwards I went to the study to wait for Peggy. I looked out of the window. The heath was no longer deserted. I saw in the strengthening light a suspiciously fit-looking man in a sports jacket, taking his dog for a walk. It was a young Alsatian in the pink of condition and showed in its movements and its split-second responses to command the infallible signs of an animal trained from birth for a definite job. In a moment of blackness I could only hope that this policeman and his dog were there to keep an eye on me and not in search of a missing child.

I took a chance and rang Julia.

'Hello, Jack.' Her tone this morning was sepulchral, yet drained of spite.

'You sound like an undertaker,' I said.

'It's a mad, violent world. Why do we put up with it?' Now her voice was even deeper and much more remote as if she were plunging down and vanishing into the earth. 'Have you heard the radio, read the papers?'

'No. No. Spare me. What are they saying?'

'Nothing you don't know already. But it all sounds so banal, so sordid, so bloody awful.'

'Go on, then.' I didn't attempt to break her mood.

'Oh, it's the same old stuff, but this time it's about the people one knows. None of you sounds real. Fitzgerald's dead, Philip's dead, Festing might die any moment, Stenton's miraculous escape –'

'What? I hate to sound selfish but how did they find out about me?'

'God knows. They do, you know, and why not? Anyway I didn't tell them.'

'Is the cricket going on, do you know?'

'There's something about a meeting. Why don't you find out yourself?' she asked.

'Don't get cross. Were you thinking of going to the cricket?'

'Yes.'

'Well, whatever happens, I'll be at the ground by eleven. Could we meet then?'

'Yes, I suppose so. Where?'

'By the nets at the Nursery End. That's always a good place.'

'I'll be there,' she said and rang off.

I turned in my chair. Peggy was standing behind me, her arms folded.

'Just tell me one thing,' she asked, 'is that affair ever coming to an end?'

'Yes. It's almost done for.'

'Are you sorry?'

I told her the truth. 'Yes and no. But more no than yes.'

Peggy perched on the arm of the chair and tapped the back of my head with her fingers as if sounding me for truth and common sense.

'You've gone pale again,' she said. 'Now, do you want to make some more calls?'

'Yes, I do.'

'Then let me make them for you.'

'All right, then.'

'I'll bring some more coffee.'

'Not for me. I'll take whisky.'

'Is that wise?' she said lightly, then, 'Yes, in your case, I suppose it might be.'

She went out and came back with the hard stuff and some cold water. Then she picked up the address book from the desk and said, 'Who's first?'

'Forester please. Try him at home. We may be lucky.'

We were. Forester sounded tired, harassed, suspicious, angry and concerned.

'Jack, Jack, my dear fellow. I'm sorry but you must know that this is not a good moment –'

'It's nothing personal,' I cut in, 'not about me, you or anyone else. Is the game going on?'

'There's a meeting in the Committee Room at nine. Quilliam will be in the chair.'

Lieutenant-General Sir John Andrews Quilliam, KCB, CB, CBE, was MCC Treasurer and himself a former President. He was a very correct old fusspot whose military career was most distinguished for his capture by Rommel six days after setting foot in the Western Desert. As it is only too easy to make fun of generals, it should be said that in the opinion of many sound judges he was reckoned in his day to be a first-rate officer whose personal courage was matched only by his concern for the men who served under him. But he had little flair for the war game and as a cricketer he was a very poor second to Sir Alec Douglas-Home.

'Will they play, in your opinion?' I asked Forester.

'Yes, I think it's highly likely. Now really, I must go and ... er ... but I would like to see you soon. I'll get a message to you. Good-bye, good-bye.'

Agitated, he rang off. There was something odd there, I thought, but no time to dwell on it at the moment.

'Please try Dr Spilsby at the hospital,' I said to Peggy who was now in a very crisp, alert and efficient mood. 'If he's not there, just ask how Reg is getting on.'

But, bright and early, Dr Spilsby was there.

'My friend,' he said cautiously and firmly, 'you're all going mad –'

'Just one of us more likely. Any ideas?'

He laughed and asked after my health and then told me

about Festing's. Reg was in a coma, still on the danger list. He hadn't, as far as Spilsby knew, said another word. 'Keep in touch,' he said, 'but keep away from hospitals.'

'Well,' I said to Peggy, 'you probably got the gist of that. Try George Abbott at home.'

He was engaged. 'Try Hunt. You know the hotel.'

Hunt, as on the previous occasion, was not available for comment.

'Then leave a message, Peggy. He may not get it but this is it. I most urgently want a word with him, at Lord's, sometime today. I'll be looking for him.'

That was done and Peggy rang Abbott again. This time he was free.

'How are you feeling, George?'

'Possibly a bloody sight better than you, this time round.'

'You rang me, remember?'

'Yes. And the question is no different now that you've joined the club. Who's trying to kill us all, for Christ's sake?'

'I don't know. Have you tried asking Hunt?'

'We speak to one another as little as possible,' said Abbott with a dry laugh. 'Why don't you have a word with the bastard?'

'I've tried, but I can't get through to him. I can't blame him entirely. I doubt if you'd be any more help in this situation.'

Abbott swore genially and then said, 'Anything else?'

'If there's any cricket will you be playing today?'

'There will be some cricket and I will be playing.'

'Great. Today, watch out for Flinders. I'll bet he curbs your natural aggression, as they say in the papers.'

'Just wait until I retire and write my memoirs. I'll give you buggers some stick.'

'You'll need a ghost to do it, George.'

'Balls. Look after yourself.' And Abbott rang off.

'That was a cheerful session,' said Peggy. 'Good old George.'

We exchanged glances and smiled. The old trust and warmth were returning and the silly side of me felt trapped again.

'You haven't touched your drink,' said Peggy.

'Nor have I.' And I took a large swig.

'Who's next?' she asked.

'It had better be Willie, I suppose. No – try Stiell first.'

'We will probably get the wife,' said Peggy. And indeed we did.

Mrs Stiell on the phone sounded quite different from Mrs Stiell in the flesh. The disembodied voice sounded waspish and thin. Her ample curves and the voice to match were apparently reserved for social occasions only.

This morning she was unfriendly and unhelpful. The doctor was over-tired and still asleep, though no doubt this absurdly early phone call had probably woken him up. I had several thoughts. Was the phone by the bed? Were they in bed together? Did they sleep in different rooms? Or was he not there at all? Or was she in bed with someone else? But I apologized and said that I merely wished to talk to him about the death of Brooke-Stanley. The dry voice crackled back like thin twigs at the start of a bonfire. She sounded unmoved and unapproachable and said that he was not in a position to speak to members of the Press. That put me in my place. I gave up. Perhaps our paths would cross at Lord's, I suggested. Then I rang off.

Peggy pulled a face, seemed to be on the point of saying something special and then changed her mind. 'Try to get Willie,' I said.

Willie's tone suggested that his usual equanimity was now being overtaken by a mood of despair. Why didn't I answer the phone? Or was it out of order, or perpetually engaged? He had been ringing since six o'clock and was now on the point of coming round. Surely, unless I was dead or unconscious, I had a duty to speak to the paper? I could only reply that surely he and the Editor must know, following Green's call to them yesterday, that under these very special and confusing circumstances, I had been asked to keep my mouth shut for the time being. And that was that. I was very sorry about it, but then, feeling sore and irritable and confused, I was also feeling a little sorry for myself. I agreed to see him at Lord's at lunch. And that if there was some cricket (and by now I had an inkling that this would be the case) then I would file copy at the end of play.

'So, for God's sake, Willie, calm down and don't come rampaging to Lord's. If I can give you a break – ha ha – I will. You know that. Meanwhile I shall keep quiet. And the more I'm pestered, the more I shall clam up.'

Willie sighed. 'Will you speak to the Editor then?'

'No. There's absolutely no point. Please give him my regards and tell him what I've told you.'

'Regards!' snorted Willie. 'That's the best yet. We'll both be out of work by the end of the week.'

'Nonsense. The best – or the worst – is yet to come. You'll see.'

At this, Willie abandoned sighing for gasping and I rang off.

As I knew that the police had spoken to Mrs Gates, I thought of ringing her but decided that such a move might cause unnecessary trouble in several quarters. That left Green. But there was no point in ringing him. I had no more to tell him right now and anyway I knew only too well that until this business was done he would never be far away. I had become indispensable to him. True, that perverse, stubborn streak in me was still as persistent as the pain in my arm. I had no intention of giving in easily but I hadn't the remotest chance of hitting myself out of trouble.

'That's all, love,' I said to Peggy. 'That must do for now.'

Suddenly I felt very tired. I sat back and sipped a little whisky, then closed my eyes for a while.

I remember thinking of the very long walk from the pavilion at Lord's to the wicket, and the even longer walk back, especially when you were out first ball. Then I dozed off but there were no dreams this time, just an impression of bells ringing and voices in the distance. Then Peggy woke me up.

'It's almost ten. When do you want to leave and where do you want to go?'

'Straight to Lord's.'

'Shall I drive you there?'

'Yes, please. In about half an hour.'

Peggy sat on the desk, swinging her legs. She handed me my unfinished drink and said, 'I think I'll join you. It's going to be quite a day.'

I looked up. 'Any more calls, anything special?'

'You might say that. There's a reception committee waiting outside the house. Some at the front, some at the back. Reporters, photographers and, for all I know, the odd policeman and assassin.'

'I see. Any problems?'

'No. I didn't let them in, of course. But I told them you'd be out eventually. There were one or two silly questions, but no bother. They seem good-natured enough.'

I yawned and finished my drink. 'What are you doing today?'

'I thought I might watch some cricket but now I've decided to come back here. And wait. And see the children . . . with the Press at the gate. If you have any trouble getting through to me, just ring next door. Mary Fulford will be in all day. She'll be glad to take a call or come and fetch me to her phone. It's all arranged.'

'Any definite news of the cricket?'

'One of the reporters says it's definitely on. But I have no details.'

When we left the house the reporters asked questions (a disorganized chaotic procedure) and the photographers went into their familiar routine of crouching down, reaching up and darting about. It took about five minutes for me to say nothing of consequence, and Peggy coped in a similar fashion. I noticed the sports coat and dog over the road and the intensification of the heath's brown parched look as the days without rain rolled by. Peggy drove down the hill to Lord's with a confident, swooping ability. Other drivers gave way to her and we stopped outside the Grace Gates just before eleven. I clambered out and slammed the door.

'I won't go on about it,' she said, 'but if that arm gets worse, see a doctor, even Stiell if you can find him. But,' she added with unusual sharpness, 'keep away from his wife. I know that bitch. She prefers all men with their trousers down ... And ring me, don't forget. And good luck.'

Peggy had shoved my dark glasses in the breast pocket of my coat. I had never cared for them much. They were, quite simply, too dark and deprived me of the sharpness of outline and the assurance of true colour that the naked eye takes for granted. But they had the superficial advantage of disguise. I put them on and began to adjust my hearing. There was a big crowd outside and a big posse of policemen too. I pushed forward, gingerly. What with my arm and my dark glasses and an undeniable touch of furtiveness, I must have resembled Cary Grant on the run in a Hitchcock movie. But the vigilant Corker on the gate recognized me immediately. He seized my arm, the bad one of course.

'Mr Stenton, sir. What a terrible ordeal. How are you keeping?'

I might have been a piece of fish on a slab that was in danger of going off.

'Not so bad. Are they going to play?'

'Yes, indeed, sir. You've just missed the announcement. Play will start on time.'

And so, for the record, on the fourth day of this Test Match, it had been decided after surprisingly short but concentrated exchanges between the cricketing authorities of England and Australia, and with approval at ministerial level, to get on with the game and to abide by its rules and conclude it, weather permitting, at the end of five days should there not be a result before then. It was a decision that caused some moaning at the bars and in the letters columns, but in the main it was a popular one. If terrorism had failed to stop the Munich Olympics why should a couple of murders stop a Test at Lord's? I made a mental note to congratulate General Quilliam when we next met, but as it turned out he was the one man who had voted to call the thing off.

Julia was waiting for me at the Nursery End. She was accepting a sweet from a bag that a small boy had thrust at her. This morning she was dressed in black with a belt of dull gold that matched her shoes. In the nets were some England cricketers including the overnight men, Branston and Byron. It was an agreeable and relaxing experience. Dedicated and professional cricketers were loosening up and knocking the ball about with grace and vigour. Byron, pausing for a moment and glancing over his shoulder, caught sight of us, pulled a face, waved his bat in recognition and hit the next ball into the car park. Instinctively I clasped Julia's hand and kissed her cheek. Her chin was cold in the mounting heat but again there was that film of sweat on her upper lip. Her green eyes were expressionless. The eyes, the window to the soul, the heart of darkness.

'Here we are, then,' I said. 'How are you feeling?'

I sounded like Corker and she looked straight through me.

'How did you find Philip?' she asked, without a trace of irony.

'With his head bashed in, probably with a bottle.'

'The Léoville-Poyferré, perhaps?'

She smiled now, darkly but not without sympathy. I was still holding her hand, and her nails, as on former and very different occasions, were biting into my palm.

'I'm going to watch the cricket,' I said.

'Me too.'

We left the nets to the sound of more cheerful clouts from the bats of Branston and Byron. How different it is when you're actually playing. We walked round the ground, stepping and sliding through the crowds. It was another full house. We stopped at the back of the pavilion. Julia looked tense and upset. It was a mood natural to her and often preceded volubility and strident high spirits. I realized the need for caution and responsibility in view of my talks with Peggy; but I could not callously let Julia drop like a stone into the water. There was responsibility here too.

'What about dinner tonight? We could go out.'

'When will that be?' she asked listlessly.

I gave her a nudge and winced. She grinned. 'How's your awful arm?'

'Terrible. Now if you promise to stay home, I'll file my copy and give them the slip. Be with you about eight.'

She nodded, then eyed me up and down.

'Goodness, you look smart today. There's no place like home.'

I had never known the Press box so crowded. There was a space next to Thirtle on the left and near to the front, the ideal position for not seeing the game very well. He waved eagerly and I responded. On my way down I noticed a strange face on the back row. A young man was sitting stiffly, trying, I thought, to solve the riddle of the scoreboard. He was wearing a dark suit and his hair was a helmet of tight curls that glowed like orange marmalade. I had seen that hair before. It belonged to the man who had been talking to the desk sergeant at the police station yesterday.

As it turned out I was glad to be alive that day for I saw one of the truly great innings of modern times. It may be true that I was due for some relief from the tension of the last four days, and it might be argued that I was only too willing to grasp at any straw and to react in a manner that grossly inflated the true value of the experience. I can only say that the relief the cricket brought me was in exact proportion to its high intrinsic merit.

It is a commonplace that the Monday morning of a Test Match normally suffers its share of the weekend hangover. There is none of the pent-up, pin-drop atmosphere of the first session on a Thursday. Batsmen, bowlers, fielders, even the captains, take quite a time to adjust to the existing tactical situation. The Australian captain, Hunt, like his opposite number, Abbott, was no great live-wire, no tactical genius, but he was tremendously sound and capable and un-flappable. God knows what depth of feelings he had about Fitzgerald but he, Hunt, was the impeccable pro and was not one to worry too much about the loss of the world's finest fast bowler, let alone our MCC President. How was it, then, that one man, without the slightest hint of planning or calculation, revealed himself the complete master of the Australian attack as the new week, overcast with cloud and misfortune, got under way?

Had Julia's party been on the Sunday night, a simple ex-planation was there for anyone to deduce. Batsmen often thrive on the relaxation of a night's boozing, whether or not they also manage to add sexual to social intercourse. Bowlers, in the same situation, tend to flatter for a few overs and then sag at the knees. But in the Australian case there was, as far as I could see, no sign of sagging or flagging. All the usual signs of Australian bounce were there, from the concerted appeals for unlikely catches to the catapult throws to the wicket-keeper from the boundary, even when the umpire had already signalled and the batsman stopped running. Only against such a standard background of the highest class is it really possible to judge the greatness of an innings.

Exceptional circumstances, extreme field placings, bad-tempered bowlers, can all come to the aid of the best of batsmen but Byron's 134 which ended on the stroke of three o'clock, just less than half-way through the day's play, was inflicted on a composed opposition who were not the least unnerved at what he was doing. In fact, there were periods when they had every right to feel pleased with themselves. Branston, when I checked with the BBC's leading TV scorer and statistician, had much more of the strike, played and missed a good deal at the swinging ball and generally kept the fields in a state of eager anticipation. The scoreboard, that advanced by 179 to a massive 329 for 1 before the part-nership was broken, was kept busy simply because Byron never missed a scoring opportunity from the first ball he received.

Byron started the day with 8 to his name, picked up in the last half-hour on Saturday night. It had been just too early for the night watchman business. Under Abbott, this was normally Rippon's job. But I knew that the acting captain, Kirkstead, never much cared for this convention, and Byron, left to his own devices, would never have wanted that sort of protection which, anyway, so often proves to be futile and self-defeating. 'There's nothing worse', Byron had once said to me, 'than to see some tail-ender trying to play like a batsman, often doing his best to run out his partner and giving the bowler a whole lot of unnecessary encouragement.'

This was an innings with no playing-in period, with none of the usual answers posed by fresh bowlers on a newly cut and mown pitch. Play the line and let anything wide on the off-side go by; restrict the back-lift for a while, remembering not to cut and hook at the same time; duck and sway away from the short balls and be prepared to take one in the ribs if there is no other way out. These are the standard defence mechanisms of the experienced player while, for want of a better description, he gets his eye in. Unlike tennis players who enjoy a knock-up on court, the Test batsman, even after net practice, is still forced to use the first few overs in the middle as a warm-up.

Bowlers, not being the fools they sometimes look, vary their own policy accordingly. On their side of the equation they don't expect to be punished if they pitch short, even with a ball 62 overs old. And so the Australian bowlers, on this Monday morning in the hot and humid conditions that had persisted all along, were merely going through the normal routine when Byron moved straight into top gear with six boundaries off the first ten balls he received. May I say that modern cricket journalism has a ludicrous fascination with such precise mathematical formulae and, much against my inclinations, it has become a habit to note the exact length and breadth of particular passages of play.

One of Byron's cover drives, replayed later on TV in slow motion as a textbook stroke to the half volley, and described as such by the commentator, was in fact nothing of the sort. The ball was a perfect length, hit on the rise with no foot movement other than a light, preliminary step nearer the line with the back foot. The poise, the balance, the swing of the bat and the judgement of length were faultless. It is one of the mysteries of batting that minimal footwork normally spells suicide early in an innings, whereas a well-set batsman can hit the ball to all parts without any apparent need for large movements forward or back or sideways. Hunt, however, was shrewd enough to realize that Byron's start was no mere flash in the pan. With the new ball due well before lunch he sensibly switched to Flinders' leg-spin and Lytton's seamers, and both had their moral successes against Branston.

Byron, on the other hand, made them look not exactly incompetent, but something even worse perhaps – terribly ordinary. Sweeps, square cuts, late cuts, and one superb straight bat pull for six off Flinders were all produced with the minimum of ostentation and with maximum effect by a master of his craft.

Unluckily I missed seeing Sobers' 254 for a World Team in Australia. It was after this that Bradman said, 'I believe that Gary Sobers' innings was probably the best ever seen in Australia. The people who saw Sobers have enjoyed one of the historic events of cricket. They were privileged to have such an experience.'

At the time I don't think I felt privileged watching Byron. Envious, fascinated, perhaps a little surprised, but no more than that. It was probably the ex-player in me made progressively insensitive by the stints of journalism.

By the time Hindmarsh and Eyre took the new ball, Byron was past his fifty and past Branston despite starting three and a half hours after him. It was then, poised for the kill, that he seemed to stand back and contemplate what he had accomplished. I don't know whether he suddenly felt perverse, or was simply taking a rest, but he definitely stepped aside and allowed the dust to settle. In fact, his was still a copy-book performance against the new ball, making sure that Abbott would not need to face up before lunch, but he had been in such total command that it was impossible not to feel disappointed when the flow was interrupted. No innings is perfect, of course, no more than a round of golf in the low sixties is perfect. Every low round ever played could be lower.

At lunch the score stood at 265 for 1; Byron 95, and Branston 80, having added only 22 to his overnight 58. There were 6 extras.

Lunchtime was a bad time, hot and hectic even though I stayed put in the Press box with a can of beer and one of Thirtle's endless supply of sandwiches. It struck me amid the din of voices and the inconsiderate questions and the sheer bloody nosiness, that lucky are they who have a Thirtle to hand. Beneath the dottiness and the seeming absorption in one subject to the exclusion of all others, there lurked the soul of tact and discretion with the support of a fastidious sensibility. He was a hard man, in the very best sense.

Willie, my Sports Editor, may have been a hard man once, but application and anxiety and the usual surfeit of journalism had made him softer than he used to be. His confidence had frayed and his judgement blunted. But his integrity like an accent transcended these details.

Ignoring my pleas to be left to my own devices Willie was sitting nearby, mournfully sipping a drink while I shouted at him without looking at him.

'I will not, repeat not, write a piece *now* on what happened to me personally, or describe my sensations (as you call them) when I found Brooke-Stanley's body at his home. And it is downright shameful of the Editor to badger you into trying to badger me to do otherwise. Today, as agreed, I will write about the cricket and nothing but the cricket.'

'Would that cover a piece about Brooke-Stanley, then?'

'No way.' I lurched into a modern idiom and caught Willie's eye. He was smiling. 'But I'll tell you what. I'll ring the Editor after I've filed my copy. What's his name, by the way? I can never remember,' I added with insolence and truth.

'Black,' said Willie.

After that we settled for a thousand words on the pure cricket and Willie left.

I looked at the heavy sky over the ground and then I looked at Thirtle.

'Bad light?' I asked hopefully.

Thirtle shook his head. 'I doubt it. I think the dark will be light enough.'

He was right. And at 2.10 it started all over again.

Branston entered another tedious, sticky patch; he was getting near seven hours in the making of his hundred. Byron needed only two scoring strokes to reach his and for the first time gave a hint of impatience at what was going on at the other end. He started to farm the strike. Once again the innings took flight revealing the ruthless artist and the master craftsman. Hunt, though unruffled, suggested that there might be an odd scratch or two on the surface of his composure. The keen edge of the Australian effort was slightly blunted. Difficult to describe but only too easy to detect had you been there.

Then, pushing the last ball of an over at just the right pace into the mid-wicket area, Byron called for a run and was answered initially by Branston. Suddenly the young Notts left-hander sensed danger. He stopped. He knew then right enough what to do. He knew he ought to go on and be run out himself but self-preservation made him turn sharply. He reached the safety of his own crease a split-second before Byron.

Branston, a picture of guilt and misery, stared speechless in Byron's direction but saw no more than the man's broad shoulders receding towards the pavilion. Byron had never broken stride, never bothered to look at the umpire. He just trotted on, in, then out of sight, taking the huge crowd so much by surprise that the richly deserved standing ovation never materialized. The greatest exhibition of faultless stroke play I ever saw was over.

In the tea interval, armed with my dark glasses, I slipped into the pavilion and up to the Secretary's office in search of Forester. No one seemed to know where he was and I was further delayed by another of those plainclothes policemen. I remember thinking afterwards of the bitter truth of the old complaint that 'they're never there when you want them'. I had a glimpse of Stiell talking earnestly to General Quilliam. A most gruesome twosome, I reflected, and felt a little stab of mischief and merriment in my heart. I was beginning to feel better – or so I believed. On my way out I was hailed and stopped by a man in his nineties. Yes, yet another old friend of my father's. And he gossiped cheerfully for a moment or two, dwelling on cricket and the glorious dead associated with the game. But he had that forgetful look in the eyes.

I managed to give Mooles the slip again and went back to the cricket. The glory had departed but there was some big hitting and cheerful clouting that delighted the crowd as Abbott (who scored a most creditable 35) pressed on with the game to assemble a big total before the close and so give England a chance of winning the match. With Byron out of the way the Australians raised both the pace and, indeed, the gaiety of their game. Flinders, not the world's greatest fielder, took a caught-and-bowled off Kirkstead that almost tore his hand off but he didn't seem to mind. And my hunch about Abbott proved right too. Pinned down by Flinders he became impatient and skied a ball to Lytton at long-off. Then Madden took a stunning catch high above his head on the square leg boundary, a ball that was really travelling. And Hindmarsh destroyed the tail with a short and quite superb demonstration of bowling first-class stuff to second-class batsmen. This included two very short balls indeed, right in line with the batsmen. I thought of Abbott again, and then Festing. This kind of bowling could never be good for the health.

Once more the game fell nicely into place at the end of a day's play. At the close, at 6.20 to be precise, when Hindmarsh bowled Standish with an amazing full toss, England were all out for 428. And so with one day's play remaining Australia needed 297 to win the match.

Without the least difficulty I sat down and wrote and filed in record time my best copy to date. It wasn't all that difficult. Byron's great shining innings was there for all to follow and in my role as a former Test cricketer rather in Byron's style, I found added zest. When I'd finished, though, I became aware that something or somebody was missing. It was Festing, of course. I missed his hovering about after the close of play and I felt rather at a loss without his irritating presence.

I was about to let myself into Julia's flat but thought better of it, pocketed the key and rang the bell. Mrs Gates let me in. It was 8.15.

'Julia's out. She's left a note. Will you have some whisky?'

'Thank you, Eileen.'

The engine in the hold had started up again, the old arm was beginning to knock. I could have done with a change of clothing. There were some clean shirts of mine in the flat but they were the wrong colour. If I changed Peggy would certainly notice when I got back home. And back home, eventually, I must certainly go.

Julia's note was brief.

'Sorry to put you out but something silly has happened. Would you come to Kettles between nine-thirty and ten? I'll leave a message for you at reception but I won't be far away.'

Kettles was a small, exclusive private hotel just off Manchester Square, near the Wallace Collection. Julia and I had once spent a night there in our early days. I sincerely hoped that she had nothing of the kind in mind for tonight. It seemed hardly likely but you never knew with Julia. Her mind was clear and logical but she did not always enjoy the consequences of her thinking and so would stimulate her sexual appetite to blot them out.

Mrs Gates, trim as a matron, brought whisky for me and sherry for herself. She sat down at the other end of the sofa and considered her drink. She looked much older today, but it was only a thought and I raised my glass and smiled at her. 'Cheers.'

'Cheers,' she responded and raised her glass as if to take a delicate sip but surprisingly almost emptied it at one go.

'Are you all right?' she asked doubtfully. 'Julia said I was to give you first aid if you needed it.'

'The whisky will do fine. Have you recovered from the party?'

'Oh that. Yes, indeed . . . I'm very sorry about all this, you know, sorry for all of you. And . . . and above all I wish I could be of more help to you and Julia. I hope you won't mind me saying this – I think I know you well enough by now – but you're by far the nicest man Julia's ever been involved with. That's in the time I've known her,' she added with a faint smile.

'Why, thank you, Eileen. Don't get in a state about it. You're supposed to be the steady one.'

Mrs Gates gave me one of those 'if only you knew' looks but she said, 'I suppose you'll be going back to your wife and family?'

'What makes you think that?'

'Oh I feel . . . I see. I draw conclusions.'

'Yes, I think you're right.'

'It's all for the best, I dare say,' said Mrs Gates, lapsing into triteness of expression but speaking tenderly.

'How is Julia, then?' I asked abruptly.

'I don't think she's sleeping very well. I don't like her being on her own.'

'Where's Polly, then?'

It was another sharp thrust.

'I'd rather Julia told you about that. I should steer clear of Polly if I were you.'

I ignored this and said, 'You can always keep Julia company for a while, can't you?'

'Yes, if she wants me to.'

Mrs Gates brought me some more whisky, then went into the kitchen.

I made two phone calls. The hospital informed me that Dr Spilsby was off duty and that there was no change in Festing's condition.

At home Peggy answered at once. There had been several phone calls, all quite manageable and of no importance. And someone had taken her picture when she poked her head out of the door. Hester had done the shopping. The children also – and much to their delight – were photographed coming through the gate. They were well. Then I said I was doing fine and was going out to dinner. I would be home by midnight. Peggy took this without a tremor of resentment or dismay. She simply said, 'Take care. I will expect you when I see you.'

I thanked Mrs Gates and said good night. I caught a taxi to Kettles Hotel, arriving there just after 9.30. As I was paying off the driver I became aware of someone leaving the hotel, stopping abruptly, and then walking off very quickly. As I turned I saw a man disappearing round the corner of the street. Or rather I saw his back only. It looked familiar. Another of Green's men, perhaps.

Kettles was an elegant place with a unique blend of good taste and great comfort. There was an enormous lounge on the ground floor, a superb place for peeping or sleeping and the favourite place for a hard core of very rich permanent residents. The lobby was deserted but as I approached the reception desk an impressive lady emerged to meet me. She had dead straight, iron-grey hair and heavy, jet-black eyebrows. She had a well-shaped mouth, painted dark red.

'Good evening. My name is Stenton. Is there a message for me from Miss French?'

'Yes, sir.' She handed me a folded sheet of paper. The message said 'I'm in room 77. Come up.'

I nodded agreeably to the lady who looked straight through me. Ignoring the lift I walked up two flights and knocked at the door of 77. It was opened by Ralph Stiell.

There was the familiar smell of Black Russians. Julia was sitting by a dressing table. She was wearing a black cashmere sweater and tartan trews. She had the old sardonic look on her face. The sexual magnetism was operating powerfully again. Polly, asleep or comatose, lay peacefully in bed, exposing her splendid shoulders and long, shapely arms. It was a big, luxurious room with plenty of space for furniture. I scowled at Stiell, then at Julia and sat down in a handsome chair by the wardrobe.

'Sorry about this, Jack,' Julia said sweetly. 'We have had a little difficulty.'

I looked again at the nude, marble goddess tucked so neatly between the sheets. In the silence I could hear her breathing. Deep but steady.

'She'll be all right in a day or two,' said Stiell. 'But she mustn't be left alone. I can get you a first-class nurse, tonight if you wish.'

'Tomorrow will do,' said Julia. 'Say nine o'clock sharp. I'll put my feet up and see the night out. I must get to the game tomorrow.'

Stiell sighed petulantly. 'I'll be at home if you need me.'

He picked up a briefcase in rich leather. His little black bag, I presumed. He turned to me and waited as if expecting me to speak.

I said nothing.

'I'm sorry I wasn't available when you rang so very early this morning. Did you need my professional advice?'

'Yes, in a manner of speaking. But it doesn't matter now.'

Julia lit another cigarette and Stiell coughed. 'It would be a good idea if you cut down on the smoking,' he said to Julia, 'it is certainly not good for the patient.'

149

'Thank you for your help, Ralph,' Julia said sweetly. 'I'll ring you when the nurse comes in the morning.'

Stiell managed an awkward smile that just embraced both of us. He looked at his watch. 'Right then, I'll be off. Good night.'

He left, closing the door very quietly behind him.

I took off my coat and folded my arms. 'What the hell's going on?'

Julia crossed her trousered legs and peered at me through the smoke.

'Have you had dinner?' she asked.

'No, of course not. I had a couple of drinks with Eileen.'

'We can eat here in the room. I'll order something in a minute.'

In the street below someone laughed uproariously. Julia stubbed out her cigarette.

'I told you that I found Polly in bed with a man. It was here. Lover-boy left and so did I. But I came back later. Polly meanwhile had fixed herself a nice little meal of drugs and drink. She was very, very unconscious, breathing heavily, making an awful racket, in fact. She looked like death. I did the best I could and luckily managed to get hold of Ralph immediately. He was round here in minutes, did his stuff, and probably saved her life. Tonight was his second, maybe third, visit. And the hotel provided some excellent, temporary nursing assistance. They know me very well here.'

I nodded bleakly. She gave me one of her sympathetic, pitying looks.

'Poor darling,' she said, and lifted the phone to order supper.

'What's the explanation?' I asked.

'Who knows? Lots of things perhaps. A need for attention, the murders, me, you, a voice in her ear . . .'

'She may have been very frightened.'

'I doubt it. Oh, she can be afraid all right, but she also

can be a calculating little sod. Her timing is good, she never lacks a sense of occasion. I shouldn't waste much sympathy on her. By the way, did you make a pass at her at the party?'

'No.'

'I believe you, not that you wouldn't mind having her. I've seen you look at her the way you look at me sometimes.'

I let that one go and then she said, 'It's turning out to be a lurid, poisonous little tale, isn't it?'

'What is?'

'Oh, all of it – since the time Fitzgerald died.'

'I have a strong conviction that it all began a little earlier than that.'

'Indeed. That sounds intriguing.'

I fired the gun.

'What about the postcards of Nottingham Castle?'

'What about them? I have seen such things,' she said evenly.

So I told her of my conversation with Brooke-Stanley and how his talk with Fitzgerald at Nottingham had first made him aware of the existence of these childish threats typed on the back of coloured postcards. And then I told her of my accidental discovery of one of the cards in her handbag.

She nodded appreciatively. 'That's right. Fitzgerald showed Polly those cards and then he gave them to her – at least that's her story. It seems a strange thing to have done. Then she showed them to me and . . . and I just took them away from her, that's all.'

That sounded another strange thing to do. But all I said was, 'Where are the cards now?'

'Still in the handbag. The other one was there too if you'd looked hard enough.'

'I had a flash of the Inspector Greens: 'You have suppressed absolutely crucial, vital evidence and may have landed yourself in a terrible mess. And that goes for Polly too.'

'It's very complicated.'

'Oh, stop it!'

'Don't shout,' whispered Julia, 'or you'll wake the baby. Stop what, anyway?'

There was a knock at the door and a white-haired old lady in a rusty black dress came in, pushing a trolley. It was clear that Kettles still lived confidently in the past and with profit in the present. When she left Julia began tinkering with the supper dishes. I went on doggedly. 'All I meant by "stop it" was stop playing with my feelings, your own and everyone else's. You not only have cards in your handbag, you have some up your sleeve as well. Tell me the truth.'

Julia handed me some food. 'Eat your supper. I can't tell you any more at the moment. Be patient and wait until the game is over.'

'What difference will that make?'

'All the difference.'

We ate and drank in silence. It was getting on for eleven.

Julia then rang Mrs Gates and told her she would not be home that night. Then she handed me the phone. 'Eileen has a message for you.'

'Inspector Green has rung. He would like to speak to you before you go to bed.'

'Is that all?'

'That was all he said. Apart from leaving his home number.'

I took this down, said good night to Eileen and threw the receiver back to Julia who banged it down on the cradle.

'Green is on the trail. He wants me to ring him.'

'Then carry on phoning.'

A woman answered. A pleasant, child-like voice, probably the brunette wife I had seen at the Rossetti. I heard her calling him – Hubert, I think it was.

'Mr Stenton,' said Green, 'I must apologize for disturbing you so late. Now it is no concern of mine whether you spend the night at Marylebone, St John's Wood, or Hampstead, but I really must see you before the cricket starts tomorrow. If we make it early enough then it need not interfere with your professional commitments. I thought you might prefer it if I called on you this time. But where?'

'The police station suits me fine.'

'Shall we say 8.30?'

'Yes. I'll be there. For your information, I'll be home within the hour. Good night.'

'You must have heard those arrangements,' I said to Julia.

'Yes.' She was smoking again, ignoring the health hazard to the blissfully oblivious Polly. At least I assumed she was oblivious. Perhaps she was taking it all down in her head.

'What shall I tell Green?' I asked.

It was a fatuous question but by this time I was feeling tired and an especially nagging variation of pain was operating in my arm.

'Tell him what you like, for God's sake. Do stop going on about it. Don't spare my feelings. You owe nothing to me. Now why don't you go home? I'll ring for a taxi.' And she did just that.

I put on my coat and went to the door in a huff.

'Come here,' she said and put her arms around my neck and kissed me delicately full on the mouth. 'Oh, you are a fool,' she said, 'the nicest and most attractive fool I've ever known.' I must have looked totally baffled and beaten. 'There now, come round to the flat after seeing the policeman. Don't forget it's the last day and play starts at eleven. So don't let him keep you too long. Try to be with me at ten. If he wants you to stay longer, just say no, there's a good boy.'

After succumbing meekly to these maternal attentions and still relishing the cool kiss on my lips, I paused at the open door.

'By the way, who was the man in bed with Polly?'

'Oh him. It's a wonder you didn't meet him on your way in. It was Forester.'

I was home not long after midnight. Peggy was sitting up in her housecoat, talking to Hester. I gave this faithful soul a kiss and she went up to bed leaving us alone in the sitting room, all very neat and tidy apart from the sheet music the children had scattered on the top of the piano.

I had done drinking and we sat for a while as I slowly exposed the day's events – until the close of play, that is. Apart from the brief talk with Green I made no other reference to the evening's events. And not for one moment did Peggy press me. All she did was to persuade me upstairs and then gently into a hot bath. Then she made me comfortable in bed and climbed in after me. I noticed that last night's nightgown had given way to the nude. But then it was a very hot night and women are no fools in these matters. But Peggy just gave a mighty yawn and said, 'Golly, I'm tired. Thank God it's the last day of this terrible game. I never want to see or hear of a Test Match again. You must find another job.'

Tuesday

Festing died in the night. I had this from Inspector Green who rang me around 7.30. I was feeling much better and had just left the bath and I took the call in the study.

'I'm very sorry,' he said, 'I thought you would like to know before we met.'

'Yes, indeed. Thank you. Did he say anything before he died?'

There was a pause. I assumed the policeman was thinking this one over.

'I wasn't there,' he said carefully. (As if that mattered.) 'There may have been an oath, a swear word. He died just after six.'

'Family? Relatives?'

'We failed to trace anyone.'

The pause came from me this time. Then I said, 'I suppose that makes three murders, then?'

'I should say so.'

'I'll see you at the police station as arranged – if you're still available, that is,' I added caustically.

'At 8.30, as arranged, Mr Stenton. Good-bye for now.'

I got a move on and ten minutes later went downstairs. My dress for the last day of the proceedings (as far as the cricket was concerned) was formal, severe, even funereal: dark grey suit, white shirt, black silk tie, black leather shoes. Peggy, fully dressed, was standing by the breakfast table and looking out of the window. I told her about Festing but we exchanged few words over breakfast. Then I followed her dutifully to the car and we drove down the hills to the police station, arriving there with several minutes to spare. We had both noticed a leisurely pursuit by two cars. We were concerned that it was nothing more than the Press. We sat in the car outside the police station under the dark sky, too dark for a batsman's comfort but quite enough light to see by. We must have looked like lovers or conspirators waiting for the day to unfold, a little fearful of its consequences. Two constables came out of the station. They were laughing and passed by without a glance.

'Do you think we might have lunch?' Peggy asked. I looked at her closely. She was beautifully turned out and wearing a very sexy dress. She was back in competition.

'I wouldn't count on it. I would almost certainly let you down.'

'Then I would like to see the cricket after lunch, until the end. Hester will see to the children after school.'

'Fair enough. There will be a ticket for you on the gate. You can rely on it.'

'I'll be there. But Jack . . . you might spare me a moment when the game's ended. Surely you could manage that?'

'Certainly. Back of the pavilion as soon as I can make it.'

I left her and went into the police station.

Inspector Green was in his clean but dreary room with its scarred linoleum, talking to the young man with marmalade hair I had seen in the Press box. Green appeared to be wearing a new suit that was not a perfect fit. Had there been a flower in his buttonhole you might have thought he was going to a wedding.

'Good morning, Mr Stenton, you are prompt as always. May I introduce Detective Constable Murchison.'

'Ah yes, the new recruit to the Press box.'

I shook hands with him. 'You don't play cricket, I hope?'

'Very occasionally, sir.'

He left the room. I sat down. Green sat down. We glowered at one another. Green had a good, bold stare but knew when to withdraw it. He fiddled with a pen and looked down at a blank sheet of paper.

'Do you doodle?' I inquired politely.

'Sometimes. Squares, triangles, circles, that sort of thing.'

I tried to relax on the uncomfortable chair but felt my muscles tightening. I was resisting, I believed, that familiar mechanism of defiance and anxiety that had characterized all my dealings with Green. He seemed to sense all this and said, 'I'm sure you would have felt more at ease, you know, somewhere other than this place.' And he waved an arm at our surroundings.

'I'm sorry,' I said humbly, 'but – and don't get me wrong about this – I didn't want to be taken off my guard.'

'Understood. Now let's try to get this business over as quickly as possible. It really is too hot for this sort of thing. This time perhaps you might be a little more forthcoming?'

I tried an innocent look. Then Green came clean.

'We now believe three men to have been murdered. And that, most likely – but here we must be careful – an attempt was made to murder you. Certainly it was an assault with a deadly weapon. I suppose you are still convinced that this person was trying to kill you?'

'What else?'

'Well, something short of actually bludgeoning you to death. A severe beating-up, perhaps, a nasty warning?'

'I don't follow.'

'Nor do I, frankly. But it has been suggested, merely suggested, that this was not a serious and calculated effort to kill you.'

'It seemed obvious enough to me. But I don't see where this is getting you.'

Green tapped his pen on the desk. 'There may be more than one person involved. Two murderers, perhaps. Or one murderer and another person, with quite different motives, who attacked you.' I had nothing to say about this and after a pause Green continued: 'Now I must ask you again, Mr Stenton, if you have any idea of the identity of the murderer or murderers of these three men, all of whom were known to you personally.'

'I have no idea.'

'Then have you a *suspicion*, a subtle difference but a valid one?'

'It sounds like playing with words to me,' I replied.

Green looked put out and I had a flash of sympathy for him. I had a picture of a life spent talking to dolts, cretins, drunks, petty criminals and irate traffic offenders. And a fat lot of help I had been in this context of violence and bloody murder. I leaned forward and said, 'At random, then. Off the cuff. I have thought that Hunt was the man who killed Fitzgerald; then I thought – for God knows what reason apart from hating fast bowlers – that Festing may have been responsible. Then – how crazy can you get – I thought that Brooke-Stanley might have murdered or more likely arranged the murders, of both Fitzgerald and Festing and that the old boy was trying to lead me down the garden path. Now he's dead and it doesn't make any sense. If you add to that lot Dr Stiell, Forester and the umpire Kite, you have the sum total of my raving and quite unjustified suspicions.'

Green appeared to listen gratefully to this modest outburst. Then he said, 'Why Kite?'

'Oh he's the flimsiest suspicion of them all – a mere suspicion of a suspicion. But he is a man of law and order, scrupulously fair but highly emotional if you know him. This could make him less than "fair" perhaps. And he feels very strongly in his circumscribed, professional world about thoughtless, vicious and potentially lethal fast bowling – rather as Festing did. So do many others, of course. You're a cricketer, Mr Green. You must know that at present the world has a vintage crop of fast bowlers. They make for a heady brew and they always will. But there's one more thing about Kite. He had a nervous breakdown a few years ago and did not officiate for a season. After that he was promptly restored to the first-class list for he is simply the most experienced and highly regarded umpire in world cricket.'

Green dropped his pen and it rolled under the desk. We both left it there. 'Francis,' he said suddenly, 'Brooke-Stanley's man. Is there any reason, that you know of, to suppose that Francis might have been blackmailing Mr Brooke-Stanley?'

'The mind boggles. No reason whatsoever. Have *you* any reason to believe so?'

Green fluttered his hands, then used one of them to pick up his pen.

'I'm asking the questions, Mr Stenton.'

'Oh sure, the same old one-way traffic.'

'That's rather unfair, Mr Stenton.'

I was about to agree with him when there was a knock at the door and a uniformed sergeant came in and handed Green a note.

'Excuse me, I'll be back in a moment.' They both left.

He was away for fifteen minutes, maybe more. My resistance flowed back. Was this part of a softening-up process, a deliberate ploy to make me nervous and angry and so vulnerable and rash, or was it just thoughtlessness or sheer bad manners? I was thinking of getting up and going out and asking what was going on when Green came back.

'I'm sorry to keep you waiting so long. Some other business.'

I didn't believe him. He was carrying a cup and said with an effort at a joke, 'I didn't bring you any tea, or coffee.'

'Most considerate of you.'

Then Green was off like a rocket.

'We know that you have been living, off and on, with Miss Julia French and that both of you are friendly with Miss Polly Parsons. We believe that Miss Parsons had intimate relations with Fitzgerald at a Nottingham hotel, and that Miss Parsons has recently spent a night with Mr Forester at a Marylebone hotel. We know that she is there now and not very well and that arrangements for her care and supervision have been made by Dr Stiell acting under the instructions of Miss French.'

'You have been very busy.'

'We can't help thinking you know that these two ladies may be involved in the murders, or at least one of them. And I'm appealing to you now, with special reference to Miss French and Miss Parsons, to help us and to tell us what you know. It's most important.'

It certainly was. I struggled with my conscience – a pretty sickly one, I must confess. Should I tell him about the postcards? They might prove to be the key to the entire mystery. 'Tell him what you like,' Julia had said. This was scarcely a plea to me to keep my mouth shut at all costs. Perhaps she was hoping I might tell Green because for some obscure reason she couldn't or wouldn't. And above all, was yet another person's life in danger? Why should the killings stop now?

Green read my thoughts, not such a difficult process as I had once imagined. He said, 'There may be another attempt at murder. There may be a lunatic on the loose and someone, as is often the case, may be protecting him – or her. It makes for a very difficult situation. There is more to be known and we must find out what it is – as quickly as possible.'

'Do you know about the postcards?' I asked.

His puzzled look failed to mask the keen interest in his eyes.

'No. What, whose, postcards?'

'You must ask Miss French about those. You really must. I'm not sure that I know the full story. I'm sure she won't deny their existence.'

Green gave me a very long and careful look indeed. I sensed that he believed what I was saying but suspected that I was holding something back. Or maybe he was just baffled. Looking back on it now, with a special wrench of memory I can see that more than one of us were not putting ourselves out to help the police with their inquiries.

'Are you betraying a confidence?' he asked.

'Not really,' I replied truthfully. 'What's more I'm sure

you will find Miss French at home this morning – say between ten and ten-thirty. I shall probably escort her to the cricket match.'

'What about the third woman, Mrs Gates?'

'I should think she's as good as gold.'

'She is certainly very protective and,' he added cautiously, 'very attractive. Does she have any lovers?'

'I should think so. I should hope so. Is it relevant?'

Green put his pen on the pad. We walked to the door. 'Sex, jealousy, money, fear, failing powers, desperate remedies . . .' He may have been trying to answer my question or perhaps he was just talking to himself. At the desk Murchison was chatting to the sergeant. As we passed by I saw that the eyes beneath the orange hair and eyebrows were cold and blue like ice.

'Make a good nursemaid, that chap,' I said to Green.

'Funny you should say that. He's very fond of children. Teaches them judo.'

Green accompanied me out of the station and we stood together on the steps. The light had improved and the irrepressible heat was pounding away.

'Do you want a lift anywhere?' asked Green.

'No, thank you.'

Neither of us moved. We were blocking the doorway and asked to stand aside to let some more policemen out.

'Why do policemen in plain clothes always look more like policemen than those in uniform?' I asked.

'Oh, they don't, you know. You've just got policemen on the mind.'

I walked down to the street and he followed me.

'There's just one more thing,' he said – and then he surprised me.

'Are you familiar with Robertson-Glasgow's essay on Walter Hammond in the 1942 *Wisden*?'

'I can't say that I am.'

'I was reading it in bed last night.'

'Not, I trust, to your long-suffering wife?'

I had a sudden vision of cricket literature as a prelude to marital bliss.

'I have memorized the end of that essay – quite an easy feat for me, I might say . . .'

He paused. Shyness or cunning?

'Well, go on then. Let's hear it.'

'He said of Hammond,' said Green, staring hard at a child on a tricycle wobbling on the edge of the pavement, 'that "he is the greatest cricketer of this generation, not merely in centuries, in the taking of wickets, and in the making of catches, but in his attitude to the game which he, while drawing from it his fame, has enriched with a grace, a simplicity and a nobility that may never be seen again".'

The child restored to safety by its mother pedalled on furiously.

'Very good, Mr Green. What a pity you will never be able to write like that about a member of your own profession.'

'Or you about one of yours, if I may say so.'

I laughed. 'Have you ever scored a century, Mr Green, anywhere, any time?'

'Alas no. I once scored 77 – not out.'

'That's not bad. I frequently came to grief around the 77s. But I never dawdled in the 90s.'

Then Green, almost absent-mindedly, shook my hand. 'Have a good day. I hope all goes well. Don't, please don't, do anything foolish. There is plenty of help around you. I'll be seeing you.' And he went back into the police station, pausing at the door to give me an emphatic nod, rather like the ghost that intends to return at a later stage in the play.

I walked slowly to Julia's place. It was hotter than ever, the pavements baking, the roads steaming, the traffic snarling and thousands on the move. What I saw without and what I felt within turned the sweat cold at the base of my spine. This was it. We were approaching the grand climax, the last act of the five-day tragedy Test Match. A small pressure group from the dead were weighing on my mind.

Perhaps they needed another to join their company before they could rest in peace.

I rang Julia's bell. She answered promptly. She was wearing the tartan trews but had removed the black sweater and also her bra. It was a disturbing sight and I said, 'Do you usually answer the door in this fashion?'

'Oh, I knew it must be you. Anyway, what does it matter? I'm about to have a bath and change. I'll be about twenty minutes. There's a bottle of champagne in the kitchen. I've just opened it. Pour some out and bring me a glass in the bath. I'm exhausted.'

I did as I was told. Julia in the bath with a cap on her head was sitting upright and soaping her breasts. I handed her the glass and turned away.

'Stay and talk to me.'

'I'd rather not. Just get a move on and get dressed.'

'Coward!' she shouted to the accompaniment of her piercing, nervous laugh.

Sensibly I ignored this and by the time I was in the sitting room and reaching for the phone I had controlled the habitual flash of desire.

I rang Forester's private number at Lord's. His secretary answered. He was out of the room. I left a message. She willingly agreed to leave a ticket for Peggy at the gate and promised that she would give it to Corker personally.

I rang the office. Willie was there. He congratulated me on my copy but sounded depressed. I told him I intended to stick in the Press box all day.

He said, 'It's really getting me down at last.' I said, 'Hang on, it won't be long now.'

I was about to ring off when he said mournfully, 'That was one hell of a chat you had with the Editor.'

Horrors. I had forgotten. 'It went right out of my mind,' I said.

'Is he there now?'

'He is.'

'Then put me through.'

'What are you going to talk about?'

'I'll think of something.'

Willie groaned and there was a succession of clicks and buzzes and voices.

'Black.'

Bruce Black, the Editor, had an impressive voice. A fine bass, not to be hurried. He would have made a superb Sparafucile, the hired assassin in *Rigoletto*. All sport bored him stiff, apart from horse racing, but he was a seasoned pro at his own game and ran some very good sports pages.

'I won't keep you,' I said recklessly and quickly but even so he managed a sarcastic growl before I went on. 'You know that I've had some pressing personal problems where this cricket match is concerned. I can only say that I hope they will end when the game does and then I'll come in to see you and . . .'

'Tonight would suit me fine. What time can you get here?'

'Oh, late.'

'I shall be here until midnight. Do look in for a change.'

'I will, then. I'll be along. By the way, Willie has been marvellous –'

'Yes. Yes. Our Features Editor will be here tonight. He has some very good ideas where you are concerned. We could start a series on Saturday.'

'Yes, I suppose so.'

'I'm sure so.'

I took advantage of the pause and said, 'Did you have a bet on The Godmother last Thursday?'

'Yes. Didn't you?'

'No. I meant to. What happened? I forgot to look.'

'She won at 14–1. Good-bye.'

Black rang off, the tone of his farewell sounding a note of utter lack of confidence in my ability as a reporter and my vigilance as a punter.

I rang Peggy, thinking she might have gone home. She had. I told her about the ticket and confirmed that I would meet her, if only for a short time, after the game.

'How was Mr Green?'

'Very fair,' I replied. 'In the end I told him more than I had intended to, but possibly less than I should – if you follow me.'

'Yes, I do. How are you feeling?'

'Pretty fair. God, it's hot.'

'God bless you.' She rang off.

The demonic phone, stirred into life, began ringing. I answered and a muffled voice asked to speak to Miss French. 'Who is that?' The caller replied with the dialling tone.

Again the phone. It was Willie. 'Jack, since we spoke we've heard that Kite is ill and unable to stand. Do you know anything about that?'

'No, I don't. I'll try to find out. Mr Black didn't sound too cheerful.'

'He's just spoken to me. He says you seem interested only in horse racing.'

'I only wish I was. I wish I had been. Sods I have cut on the turf.'

'What's that?'

'Never mind. Later. Cheerio.'

I went into the kitchen and brought back the champagne and two clean glasses. It was nicely timed, for Julia came in, dressed to kill in a white silk dress resting on the knee and again with those silk stockings with their slightly heavy, sensual look. The hair looked careless but all the better for that and the make-up emphatic but discreet. She looked very beautiful and tired and tense. I poured out the rest of the wine into the ample glasses.

'I told Green about the postcards. Just the mere mention of them. And I told him he must talk to you about them. He's still in the dark, you know.'

'Aren't you?'

'Totally.'

Julia began smoking and we were very quiet for a time. Then she rang Mrs Gates. Very brief, very practical.

'How's Polly?' I asked when she put the phone down.

'She'll live. The nurse is most attractive. Stiell must have done that on purpose.'

She frowned, lifted her glass and said, 'Well here's to the last day.'

The phone again. 'Speaking,' said Julia. 'What can I do for you, Mr Green?'

It was a difficult conversation to follow. I didn't get the thread of it and for some strange reason my mind drifted back through the years when I was playing on a very nasty wicket at Portsmouth, a green-top. There was a fast-medium bowler called Hopwood. He wasn't the greatest but he was always dangerous for a few overs at the start and a positive menace if the conditions were in his favour. There were only two men and two dogs watching that morning. I simply couldn't bring myself to fight it out. Why the hell, I thought, play the hero and risk a thick ear. Sometimes when you can't cope with that, you hit out. That's what I did at Portsmouth . . . And I got out, too, hooking desperately at a short ball and giving an easy catch to square leg. That was a relief. Why on earth had this come into my mind?

'Wake up,' said Julia. She had finished her talk with Green and was drinking the last of the champagne. 'It's too late to make love now. It's time we went to the ground.'

It was hard going at Lord's. Outside the Grace Gates, in an atmosphere of barely manageable chaos, were television crews, photographers, reporters, a big police contingent and a surging mob. I put on my dark glasses and Julia crammed a floppy white sun hat on top of her flaming hair. We became an immediate centre of attraction. I seized her hand and with a combination of muscle and bad language (and the help of the police) forced a way into the ground. I lost my glasses, Julia her hat, and one of her magnificent silk stockings was torn.

'That's a pity,' I said. 'Now your legs are ruined.'

'I have another pair of stockings in my bag.'

I had a vision of Nottingham Castle.

'The things you keep in that bag. Will you never learn?'

I acknowledged a mournful wave from Corker and then steered Julia into the path of General Quilliam. He was viewing the scene with intense displeasure and he looked at us in pretty much the same way. But to be fair he didn't let the side down. He bowed stiffly to Julia and gave me one of those classic, limp handshakes.

'A terrible business,' he said vaguely. 'It's probably all the fault of television. We should have stopped the game at the end of the first day. No one would listen to me.' He glared at us as if we were entirely to blame for all that had happened. It did cross my mind that this was as good an explanation as any, but I said quietly, 'There may be something in what you say, sir.' We left him.

If anything, inside the ground was worse than outside. There was muttering and cursing and bumping and barging. We got to the Members and Friends enclosure. With her back to the stand, Julia pulled up her dress and ripped off her damaged stocking, threw it away and replaced it with another one from her bag.

'That's that,' she said.

I looked at my watch. It was 10.45.

There was a pause, a moment of awkwardness. Her dark green eyes were smouldering with concern and disturbance, and a hint of fear. She looked childish and a little mad.

I had an overwhelming desire to take her out of this place and away from it all, to take her home, to call Mrs Gates, to enforce some peace and rest on that troubled mind. But instead she clutched me tightly and said, 'Go home, Jack. It doesn't matter any more. Go home now.'

People in a hurry broke us apart. I can't remember what I said but she was swept away from me and up the staircase and into the stand. The dread returned with renewed force. Sick with dread – for the first time in my life I realized the true meaning of the words. I went to the Press box.

Thirtle, faithful as ever, had kept my place for me and I joined him as England took the field. I looked at the umpires.

Filbert, yes, but no Kite. In his place I saw the tall, stooping figure of a former county cricketer, Frank Beech.

'What's happened to Kite?'

'I'm not sure,' said Thirtle. 'No one seems to know. And now there's a rumour that Reg Festing is dead.'

Festing. I'd forgotten all about him. Never mentioned it to Willie. Another black mark. 'Yes, Festing's dead. He died around six this morning.'

'God in heaven,' said Thirtle.

I glanced behind me just in time to see Murchison slipping into the box to stand at the back. Then Hunt and Burnett walked out to open Australia's second innings and the last of the match. Australia with ten men to bat needed 297 to win. Play this day was from eleven to five-thirty, but either captain could claim an extra half an hour and so extend the game to six. The heat seemed to be the worst yet but the light was middling to good and if the rain held off I knew in my guts that we would see a battle royal.

At the Nursery End, by the sightscreen, I could see the weatherbeaten Merryweather squatting on his haunches. At the Pavilion End, Standish was preparing to bowl to Hunt. The crowd's murmurs died away. There was one great shout and then Standish turned to begin his run.

At this moment, in spite of the very special tensions of this last day, I don't think there was ever much doubt in the players' minds that it would all end in a draw. I am sure the dead as well as the living would have settled for this. After all we had been through, a draw seemed the best and most inevitable outcome. But the media, with the understandable intention of squeezing a unique situation dry, had built up the more dramatic alternatives of victory and defeat. Here, after all, was the last act of a melodrama, still pregnant with violence and the threat of even more unknown and terrible things to come. Millions would be looking and listening and reading. Like sightseers flocking to a disaster area, thousands had jammed the approaches to the ground and many were trying to bribe, even fight, their way into the ground. It was a bad day on the Stock Exchange and the pubs were running out of beer.

Perhaps murder would out but meanwhile the cricket was pursuing its own destiny. Nine good deliveries could mean the beating of Australia. One, or two, effective batting partnerships could spell defeat for England. Much depended on how flexible the captains were prepared to be. If there was to be a winner, the odds were probably on England, because on a pitch five days old, 9 wickets are usually easier to come by than 297 runs.

Abbott, back in charge, was banking on an early breakthrough, knowing that the Australian tactics must be aimed at preserving wickets up to lunch. By the same token, close-set fields meant pickings for the Australian openers, even without taking undue risks. Hunt and Burnett played soundly and without inhibition. What chances they gave never went to hand and they proceeded to take the edge off the England attack. At one o'clock the openers had scored 95 and were beginning to show, from an England point of view, the first ominous signs of really going for the runs. It was a crucial moment for the fielding side, still without success in the unusually long stint before lunch. Abbott was probably cursing the convention that advances play on the fifth day of a Test Match for no better reason than to assist travel arrangements for the players to the next match.

I had been studying Hunt through my glasses. The Australian captain was unwinding nicely. The slight marks of strain in his face were beginning to dissolve, just as the wrinkles of frost leave the earth when the sun is up. Then Standish, who had troubled Hunt least, was recalled by Abbott to make a final effort before lunch. Hunt let the first ball go by, then square-cut the second with great majesty and authority. It was a truly magnificent stroke. It looked good and sounded even better. But Byron, in the gully, with an intuitive act of anticipation, had already moved to his left, thus gaining an extra yard on his way to the ball. He made the catch look so easy that half the fielders and the

T.–8

whole of the crowd were, for the second time in the match, dissuaded by Byron's coolness and poise from any exultant clapping. They responded, as Hunt walked immediately, with one of those celebrated, stunned, disbelieving silences. Byron made light of the performance by flicking the ball nonchalantly away into an empty space and began rubbing the side of his left knee, as if further to distract from the catch itself. A touch of arrogance, perhaps, but maybe a twinge of pain as well.

Maitland came in and Abbott, conventional and sensible, almost screened him from view with a closer than ever field of extreme hostility. But just as it is possible to hook a salmon when only casting for trout, it was Burnett who landed himself in the net. He was facing Mappleton who had bowled well in this innings, but without luck. His ball to Burnett was of good length, straight and maybe a little below his usual pace. Burnett, it seemed to me, tried to hit this one for six over mid-off but he got his equations all wrong and gave Abbott a sharp but sure catch at cover.

Madden came in to join his colleague from New South Wales. They had a brief chat, if only to express surprise at meeting one another again in the space of five minutes. They played easily enough until lunch when the score was 110 for 2.

At lunch I stayed put. I had thought of trying to see Abbott and Hunt for a moment but concluded that they had problems enough without my adding to them. No one bothered me. I had a beer and a sandwich with Thirtle and received two notes by messenger. One from Forester asked me to meet him in his office as soon as play started after lunch. He apologized for the timing, but that was the best he could do. The other from General Quilliam, though more in the nature of a command than a request, suggested a meeting in the Committee Room during the tea interval. I was able to confirm these arrangements over the internal phone system. Murchison still stood quietly at the back. A little after two I went to see Forester. It was hard work for such a short trip but the crowd was still swarming and the entrances to the pavilion were closely guarded. I made it on time but Forester didn't. I waited for five minutes, recalling the other occasion a few days ago when I had reacted uneasily to the sound of that light, athletic tread which turned out to belong to Brooke-Stanley. Then Forester appeared, a little dishevelled and out of breath. He began to apologize but I cut him short.

'Take it easy. What's the rush?'

He began fiddling with bottles and glasses.

'It's pink gin, isn't it?'

'That will do fine.'

His hands were shaking slightly but he didn't need a drink to steady them, just a moment to sit down and get his breath (and maybe his nerve) back. He fingered a silver-framed picture on his desk. The back was towards me. Not a wife. Father, mother, brother killed in the war, a dog?

'Jack, I've had some most disturbing conversations with the police.'

'Welcome to the club.'

'Don't get me wrong,' he said peevishly, 'but all these terrible things, it seems to me, always come back to you.'

'A sort of focal point of infection, you mean?'

'I'm not sure what I mean,' he said hoarsely, 'but how do you think the police found out that I had spent the night with Polly at Kettles?'

It struck me then for the first time. Polly put the kettle on. I kept it back.

'You are a fool. They've been watching a bunch of us since Fitzgerald died.'

'Why would they do that?'

I wasn't entirely sure of my ground but I said, 'Simple. Festing, poor meddling old sod. He put them up to it. Maybe not such a bad idea as it's turned out.'

'I must confess, I must tell you,' he said, putting a hand over his eyes, 'I told them that you were the person they should talk to. I wasn't accusing you, of course, but quite frankly I couldn't think of anyone else, or indeed, of anything else to say.'

There was a great roar from the crowd. Caught unawares, we both pricked up professional ears.

'What did Polly tell you?' I asked.

He replied with a despairing wave of the arm. 'Nothing that I can recall. We were both drunk and making love.'

'No more than that?'

'Well, yes. Afterwards she did say she thought you were a bad influence on Julia.'

I thought a moment, then said, 'She's quite a girl, our Polly. What's she like in bed, by the way?'

'Spare me that,' he said shortly.

'Surely she didn't try to kill herself because of you?'

'God, no.'

He looked at me with the true face of despair.

'She's tried it on before, you know, with another man.'

'How do you know that?'

'He told me himself.'

'And who was he?'

'Fitzgerald.'

That took me by surprise. That one really got through me. Forester looked dejected but the colour had flowed back into his cheeks. What could I say?

I said, 'Tell me some more.'

'It was after the MCC game. There was a party afterwards at their hotel. Nothing very special. There were some girls there, Polly certainly and possibly Julia. He reckoned that he had Polly lined up for the tour, boasting and swaggering a bit; you know the sort of thing, a bit coarse but fairly normal.'

Yes, I did know that sort of thing. Only too well. Who was I to judge?

'Then at Nottingham,' Forester went on, 'they had a night or two together. And there was something else, I don't quite know what, that had upset him very much. Anyway, he woke up in the night and found all the lights on and an empty pill bottle by the bed. He found her in the bathroom and she was still conscious and he made her sick, quite easily. He had caught her in time, just as she meant to be caught perhaps. She said afterwards it was only a game and she often did things like this when she had been drinking and making love. Then he told me that she had stolen something from him and that there was a conspiracy to kill him.'

I shook my head in disbelief yet I believed every word he was saying.

'But when, when, for Christ's sake, did he tell you all this?'

'On the Wednesday. The day before he died.'

'Forester, you're in it up to your neck – but no more than the rest of us, I suppose. But for God's sake, man, knowing this and believing it, why did you go to bed with her at Kettles?'

He stood up and knocked his glass over.

'I couldn't help it. I just couldn't help it.'

I saw the pain and the strain in his weak, essentially good-natured face.

'What shall I do?' he asked.

'Wait until the game's over. Who killed Fitzgerald, by the way?'

'I don't know.'

'And the others?'

'It's beyond me, I'm too confused. And,' he added with a twisted smile, 'I'm probably ruined. It's all so unbelievable.'

'Not if you use your imagination. I'll see you around.'

I believe I gave Forester a comforting smile as I left him but I felt far from comfortable inside. There seemed to be no end to the ramifications of these dark and preposterous forces that had already caused the death of three people. Certainly in the case of Fitzgerald he had not exactly kept quiet about his fears and the threats to his life. He had managed, among others, to confide in both the Secretary and President of MCC. Not bad going. In the end it might turn out that a whole cricket team had known and that, like Forester and Brooke-Stanley, they either ignored the information or laughed it off, or waited curiously to see what would happen. Once more I forced my mind back to the cricket and returned to the Press box.

Maitland and Madden were still there, batting steadily and with care but with a pleasing, jaunty touch now and then. How much of this was bluff and how much due to a genuine conviction that the runs could be made was anyone's guess. Either way it had the effect of an early bowling change and many minor alterations of field. There was still no hint of real urgency on either side but as the time went by, the responses back and forth became more sensitive, more easily triggered. Mathematically, it began to look as though the two sides were set on something of a collision course. The captains could still afford a waiting game, but, given the way things were going, emergency action would be forced on one or the other before long.

The sinking of the liner *Andrea Doria* flitted across my mind. She was rammed by the *Stockholm* on 25 July 1956, only a matter of weeks after my parents had sailed in her. It was one of their party pieces. Two huge, modern ships, each lured, it seemed, into fatal embrace by the mere presence of the other, each turning implacably towards the point of impact, when a straight course from either would have meant open water between them. Then another wicket for England brought me back from the vicinity of the Nantucket lightship to the more confined space of Lord's.

Madden, restless and eager, seemed to fancy his chance with Ackroyd who had been bowling rather short, but like Burnett before him he completely mistimed his stroke and struck the ball into Kirkstead's huge hands at mid-wicket. 180 for 3. Another quick wicket and we would be in business. Well, it wasn't all that quick but it came sharp at four o'clock. It was the new batsman, Musgrave, and he looked in no trouble at all. Then Ackroyd again. As I have said before, the Lord's Press box is not the best place to make an lbw decision. But there was Musgrave, playing well down the wicket to Ackroyd and missing (maybe flicking?) a ball that went onto his pad. I seem to recall that only Ackroyd appealed and then none too confidently. But umpire Filbert gave the matter long and agonizing consideration, then slowly raised his hand. By this time I had my glasses on Musgrave. The third and most dashing of the trio from New South Wales looked appalled, then outraged. He struck his bat violently on the ground, then began a steady, seething walk back to the pavilion. Lytton came in and took his time about it. The tea score was 205 for 4. Australia, with just short of one and a half hour's play remaining, needed 92 to win with 5 wickets in hand.

The cricket had reached a tantalizing stage – and so had the betting. The bookmakers, whose business depends less on the accuracy of their predictions than on the size of their margins, still made a draw a clear favourite at 4–6 on, with Australia at 6–4 and England 2–1. I noted wryly that these figures constituted a colossal 33 per cent overround book against the punters. Some business. And in cricket there are no fiddles, coups or inside information to worry about – just a simple three-card trick – win, lose or draw. Then just as my mind was straying to those daft computer matches when machines decide how many runs Bradman might make in a make-believe match against a bowler of another era, I found myself entering the pavilion and on my way to meet the Treasurer.

General Quilliam was waiting for me at the door of the Committee Room and he pounced on me rather like a commissionaire at a Mayfair theatre club who suspects that you're trying to slope in without paying. Under the polite, curious eyes of his colleagues and friends (including one or two of mine) he dragged me into a corner and produced, as if from his coat tails, a glass of Buck's Fizz.

'Your father used to like this,' he said gruffly.

This time I gave him a careful look. A touch of Sir Bindon Blood as portrayed by Sir C. Aubrey Smith. A man not dragged, but rather trudging under his own steam, reluctantly, into the second half of the nineteenth century. He had fine grey eyes and beautifully shaped nostrils.

'I was a bit short this morning, Stenton. I always am with you, of course. Never cared for your cricket much. But I read in a book somewhere – or to speak true it was drawn to my attention – that Jack Hobbs in his old age would make a special journey just to see you bat. Don't know what to make of that.'

Neither did I. I stared at him in amazement.

'I'm sorry about this business but . . .'

He lowered his voice, postponed for a moment what he was going to say as his eye fell on my untouched glass. 'Do have a drink, my boy. I got that specially for you.'

I obliged and he went on.

'You see, how can I put it, I'm not such a bloody old fool as I look. I know how fond Philip was of you. And I know in a way . . . er, how can I put it . . . that you're fond of, have been very good to Julia. There's a connection there, if only you can work it out.'

I actually tasted the second drink from my glass. It was very good indeed.

'There's no great hurry,' he said, 'at least I think there isn't. If you can bear it, come and see me next week sometime. You just can't beat this place for unfinished and unsatisfactory conversations.'

He took the empty glass from my hand and stood aside, inviting me to go, dismissing me, as it were.

But he followed me to the door and shook me rather ostentatiously by the hand.

'You'll be wanting to get back to the cricket,' he said.

Baffled by the whole interlude, I thanked him and turned away. Then his voice called after me.

'I enjoyed your piece on that innings of Byron's. Best thing I've read for years. Take care.'

I was half-way upstairs to the Press box when his last words sank in. 'Take care.' What an odd expression for an old man to use. What on earth did he mean? I had a depressing feeling that, partly out of guilt and the need for a new confidant, he was going to take me under his wing.

The number of uniformed police had increased considerably during the brief tea interval and there were two stationed by the entrance to the Press box as I hurried back. The light was indifferent and the heat and humidity unrelenting as always. Thirtle had acquired some cans of beer and put one in my place. The game started up again.

You might have thought that Maitland, now the key figure from the Australian point of view, would have shielded Lytton from the steady England pressure which was now resting on the excellent seam bowling of Kirkstead, with Rippon and the unpredictable Ackroyd in support. But Maitland, wisely perhaps, showed no such consideration and Lytton, cool but aggressive, had scored 25 when, just after five o'clock, he was bowled by Kirkstead. 237 for 5. It was one of those balls seen only at Lord's, moving a massive distance down the slope. That slope which always bothered me, falling, as it does, some eight feet from the Grandstand to the Tavern. Then Eyre came in. Now this man could bat a bit (a convincing 50 at Trent Bridge) and made most of his runs on the on-side. Without a sign of nerves he promptly dealt with Kirkstead in this fashion, with two scorching fours past mid-on. Two overs later he took 2 off Rippon, then another fine boundary with a straight drive just wide of the bowler's arm. Then he tried the same shot again and this time Rippon took a catch hard and low down, right on his boot laces. 257 for 6. Time 5.25. It was an increasingly intriguing situation. Without fuss or brilliance, the two sides were now very close, right on the point of collision. Miles away, some thunder rolled.

Now it was Roper's turn. He looked awkward and so he proved to be. Everything he did in terms of stance and stroke was horrible but he always took some shifting and seemed to advertise the fact. Even worse, he appeared to liberate Maitland who, with a century in sight, began to hit out and

177

drive back the field. Twenty runs came in ten minutes. I had my eyes on Abbott and thought I detected some bad language like people use when they are talking to themselves while shaving. Then the England captain recalled Standish and Mappleton, his best pair and his last chance. It was the sensible decision but it crossed my mind then (and still does when I think about it) that Ackroyd was the one bowler he might have persevered with.

But in Standish's first over he had Roper caught at second slip by Lyndhurst who for the second time in the game came to life and did something positive. Perhaps I should add, though, that this proved to be his last game for England. When Flinders came in to join Maitland the ground went very quiet indeed. When, some minutes later at 5.45 precisely, Flinders, after stubborn defence, was bowled by Mappleton, Lord's then went as quiet as a graveyard that has been closed to the public.

I still believe that, so riveting was the conflict in the middle, that when the last man, Hindmarsh, came in I was one of the few people to see an England player have a word with his captain, wave to the twelfth man on the balcony and then jog lamely off the field. I looked around me. The reporters were as absorbed as the rest and without pausing to think I slipped out of my seat and out of the box and down the stairs and past the policemen.

It was an absurd thing to do. I had turned my back on a situation when Australia, with fifteen minutes to go and one wicket to fall, needed ten runs to win. But then I was going to face up to the man who had just left the field. He had been on my mind for some time and right now, in the last minutes of this deadly game, I had to know the truth. Fortunately I had one warning as I reached the back of the pavilion. Once again, my arm was pounding away like the engine in the ship's hold. It was the body's message to the mind emphasizing that I was not fit and in no condition for a serious trial of strength.

The back door was unguarded. Mooles as I mentioned before had never needed much encouragement to neglect his post. Amazingly, the police were not there either. The cricket was gripping the whole community. I went upstairs, still meeting no one, and headed for the England dressing room. Then an instinct told me that the man I sought would not be there. A moment later I opened the door of the small treatment room and then closed it behind me. I was right. Byron was there alone with his back to me, taking his shirt off. He turned around.

'Hello, Stenton. Do you need treatment too?'

He was sweating but this only emphasized his superb physical condition.

He was rather like me fifteen years before, but the shoulders were a little broader, the pectoral muscles more pronounced and he had biceps like a heavyweight boxer.

'Hello, Byron. I thought you might have hurt yourself.'

'I have, actually,' he said quietly. 'My knee. I felt something go when I caught Hunt. Did you see that, by the way?'

'Yes. Out of this world.'

He draped the shirt over his shoulder, then stood very still. 'Out of this world. That's a strange expression. Did you want anything?'

He was in much better shape than I had dared imagine. He was standing quite still in a most relaxed, deadly fashion. I didn't like his dark blond hair that looked so much at home on his head and, most of all, I didn't like the fixed and watchful look in his dark blue eyes. I heard myself responding in a most roundabout way. 'It seems an odd time to ask,' I said, 'but then it may be as good a time as any, perhaps even the best time of all. Did you kill Fitzgerald and all the other people?'

He didn't budge.

'I certainly didn't kill you,' he said.

A great roar from the crowd shook the sky and rocked the pavilion.

'Why don't you go and watch the finish?' asked Byron. 'It sounds exciting.'

'We shall probably lose,' I said, watching him carefully.

'Do you think so? Well, in that case it won't be my fault. I've done my best, you know.'

Though still intensely on his guard I thought I detected a dreamy look in the eyes that were growing darker, as the sea gets darker down below.

'Did the fast bowling get you in the end?' I asked.

His powerful shoulders twitched violently and the shirt dropped off.

'Well now,' he said, 'what makes you think that? Did it bother you by the way?'

'Not really,' I replied truthfully. 'It got me out a few times, but I was never afraid of it.'

The blue eyes now were almost black. He stroked his nose. I went on talking.

'That second innings of yours should have told me the truth. Festing probably spotted it earlier than I did – the way you blossomed after Fitzgerald died. You were always king-pin at staying down the other end, away from the rough stuff, but I certainly never saw you flinch under fire. That's where you fooled us all. You must be one of those secret worriers. Lord knows, I've had nightmares myself about it.'

He appeared to take this very calmly and bent down to rub his knee. This distracted me and I lost my concentration for a moment.

'You bastard,' he said quietly, then came at me like a tiger and crashed the side of his hand right on the centre of pain on my damaged arm. As I shouted with pain he kicked me neatly in the groin and I crashed back against the door and fell down.

I seemed to recall some joke about a red mist before the eyes. The pain was excruciating but I could see him, taking his time, and picking up a heavy heat lamp. This time he was careless and I was quick. There was a blur of chrome metal as the thing descended, just grazing my head and smashing with great force against the door. Then the door broke open at my back throwing me headlong at Byron's feet. As he kicked me viciously on the head I caught his ankle and with a violent twist brought him down. Then a terrible pain rang in my ears and closed my eyes.

The way back to consciousness was revolting and painful and a great strain on the will. There was a hammer in my head, another in my arm and overwhelming nausea in the pit of my stomach. Then I was convinced that my vision had suffered permanent damage, I saw faces forming then disintegrating, the picture was blurred and the eyesight had lost its edge. Then there was gradual improvement and the images became sharper and my hearing returned to co-ordinate with my vision. There was Peggy, Inspector Green and the policeman with orange hair. One of his eyes was closed, and then I realized that so was one of mine.

I groaned encouragingly.

'What was the result?' I whispered.

Green leaned forward and told me.

'They deserved to. And what's happened to . . . to . . .' I had completely forgotten his name.

'He's been taken away.'

'Was he troublesome?'

'Very. I'm afraid his arm is broken.'

Green retired for a moment and Peggy bent forward. Beyond the ringing in my ears I was aware of another ferocious sound.

'What's that? What's that noise?'

With infinite gentleness she placed a finger on my bruised cheek.

'That's the rain,' she said, 'the greatest downpour since the flood. It all started five minutes after the game ended.'

It seemed fitting and symbolic, an act from the very heavens themselves to wash away the blood and the violence. If only the game had been a wash-out from the start.

Epilogue

Julia died in the early hours of Wednesday. This was established later when the inquest was adjourned and the body formally identified and then cremated. The eventual verdict was suicide, achieved by a nicely calculated blend of barbiturates and alcohol. To dispel any shadows of doubt Julia had left a note that was terse, uncomplicated and singularly uninformative. She wrote that she had intended to kill herself, took full responsibility and offered no explanation.

This I learned from other sources. However, she did not leave *me* without an explanation. Her letter that reached me in hospital four days after her death had the NW8 postmark. It was date-stamped first post Wednesday morning. She must have gone out for a moment to the postbox before returning to her flat to start the process of killing herself. Considering its length and its details her letter might have been the final version of a draft that she had written some days before and then hurriedly brought up to date. It was long and disturbing, but the childish character of her handwriting was as faultless as copperplate. This is what she wrote:

Darling, it may have come as a surprise to you that I have thoroughly done (I hope) myself in. You will also be surprised by my expressing myself at such length in writing. I'll never do it again, my love, I promise you. You got very cross once when I never replied to your love letters, in spite of the fact that you told me where I could reply to you safely, without disturbing the family circle. You must have thought I was a total illiterate. But what you may have forgotten was that one, just one, of the things that attracted me to you was your admission – boast rather – that in your youth you used to write other boys' love letters to their girlfriends. So bear with me now in my one and only love letter to you. It's mainly a confession, but I'm sure if you try, you will be able to read the love between the lines.

I am going to put one thing after another, in some kind of logical sequence, in the hope that by the end you can make some sense out of it. It won't, can't, be the whole truth, of course, but then there must be some pieces of the truth known only to you. Perhaps some of your pieces will fit into mine. I have become a little confused about who said what to whom. To be frank, I wasn't listening to you some of the time when you were speaking to me so urgently.

There must be more than one reason why we never really got together over this business. I take most of the blame but (strictly between ourselves) I am still sensible enough to insist on your sharing part of it. But I always *knew* more than you did. And I did have a moment in the middle of writing this (yes, I read it all through and then went back and did it all over again) when I thought I might write myself out of suicide but as you know this wasn't to be. So I'll get on with it.

I am the illegitimate daughter of Philip Brooke-Stanley. My mother was a young Australian socialite – if that's the right term – and I never knew her. Philip – I can never think of him as Daddy – was never married but he was a gay (old sense) dog and certainly enjoyed laying the young maidens. Before the boarding and the finishing schools I lived in New Zealand in total seclusion – up to a point. I was in the care of a posh old girl – a governess, I suppose – who was remarkably active and adored fishing and riding. Don't laugh, but we played cricket together with the assistance of some very tough and virile lads. I was sexually precocious and she did nothing to hinder my curiosity. She told me nothing of my past. That may have been one of the reasons why she was so keen on keeping me occupied with the present. She was very proud of her figure. And her legs, even in her late sixties, were quite exquisite and switched on the young and old alike.

After that there were the other places in France and the West Indies and, eventually, England. When I was seventeen Philip told me the truth and settled a lot of money on me to cope with it. But with one bound I must free me and you from the past and tell you (now she tells me!) that Quentin Byron was my lover for some years before I met you. I don't want to seem crude but he did have me two or three times after my affair with you started. In private he was a morose, violent man, and now, I suppose, a mad one too. But we were very discreet and I think that, Philip apart, the only person who knew was General Quilliam but he must have kept quiet. This year, as you may have guessed, Polly found out. Now you know about the problems of my sex/love life. As time has gone by (I'm twenty-nine) I have increasingly found much more sexual satisfaction with women than with men. But I had not gone too far in that direction when I met you. And so while I had you in bed, and Byron occasionally, I became infatuated with that silly, dangerous bitch, Polly. What madness. I shall be glad to be free of the sex. It has consumed me. I have always had just enough intelligence to know what was happening to me but never the character to resist it.

Then there was the drug scene. This didn't seem of much consequence at the time and can't be the explanation of what has happened now, but all the murders seem to have stemmed from it. Though, as I will try to explain in a minute, the murders were committed (I think) for an entirely different reason. Again, I don't know how much you know because we always seemed to have talked to one another without listening, but in the last England tour of Australia (you weren't there but I was) Byron and Fitzgerald became friendly in that strange sort of way, that nervous, tentative way, that world-class batsmen and world-class fast bowlers do sometimes. It's a subtle business and I know you understand it better than I do, but you've always been slow to spell it out. We were an odd, possibly disagreeable, threesome, but we had some good times together and we all smoked pot. Fitzgerald (though you may have thought otherwise) never tried to lay a hand on me until after that party in England when I slapped his face. But there was nothing doing. But Byron was quite the most possessive person I have ever known. He was a superb, hard, cruel lover and eventually drove from me all the tenderness that you managed to restore. All the time, though, Fitzgerald, for all the signs of worry, trouble with women and being anti-social, wanted above all to be the greatest fast bowler in the world. He had intense personal pride. Then in the very last Test of the England tour he turned on, for a short time only, a most alarming burst of speed that seemed quite in excess of his normal gift. You may recall that Byron was at the receiving end and had his ribs bruised before his wicket was broken. He made 47, the highest score of the innings but he was glad to be out in the end. From that time the two 'friends' became enemies. And it was on the beach, after turning in rage and frustration on me, that he told me, in a frenzied bout of love-making, that Fitzgerald's spurt of demonic energy was the result of a powerful stimulant, the kind that makes athletes jump higher and longer and throw things further, and that sends cyclists whizzing up the mountain slopes. So, obviously, it makes fast bowlers bowl even faster. And this was the trouble that Fitzgerald brought with him to England this summer.

Alongside that was the other thing that you must have twigged in the end. (For a bright person you can be awfully dim at times.) Byron, before the last Test at Sydney, dropped his guard for a minute – not in bed, by the way – and told me that he was worried. For all his brilliance and beauty and strength he was increasingly distressed by the very fast stuff. It might have been to do with the drinking bouts, rare but increasingly fast and furious, the 'mild' drug addiction, the sex drive and a progressively disturbed mental and emotional condition. But the edge had gone off his confidence and concentration; and his nerves, though outwardly firm and composed, were beginning to fray. It occurred to me that Byron's friendship with Fitzgerald had been more by way of an insurance policy, rather than a genuine liking, maybe a hope for a stay of execution.

And so we come to Nottingham, such a short time ago, but for me it seems an eternity. This was the set-up. I felt lonely and confused. I was sure I could never hang on to you for long. I knew in my bones that you would go back to your wife. This fuelled my infatuation with Polly. Like Byron she had great sex appeal and, I must tell you plainly, was extremely ruthless, proficient and effective in the arts of love. She taught me a thing or two. It was difficult to keep these things from Byron who, sensing that I wanted to be rid of him at last, promptly exploited all my weaknesses and passions. And he certainly pushed the willing Polly into Fitzgerald's bed – poor devil. Then Byron persuaded me, cunningly, to spend two nights with him at his brother-in-law's house at Newark. That was the nearest I

185

got to Nottingham apart from a brief visit before the game was abandoned. We didn't meet there, as you know, but I do recall seeing you standing in the rain and talking to Festing, Thirtle and Ransley. It was at Newark that Byron produced the post-cards and typed the messages on an old Remington long after the others had gone to bed. This was after I had refused to sleep with him. I should have realized that he had had a much more deadly plan in mind when he took my rejection so calmly. Sober as a judge himself, he got me drunk and nervous and giggly. Knowing what Polly was up to I was in no mood to feel sympathy for Fitzgerald. I went along with the game of trying to frighten Fitzgerald and then I went to bed on my own to sleep it off. Byron must have arranged the deliveries and the next time I saw the cards was in London when Polly, who had booked in at Kettles, gave them to me 'for a laugh' when I had just got out of her bed and was dressing to go home. And quite truthfully I never thought of them again until Fitzgerald hit Jarvis over the heart before lunch on Thursday. But when Fitzgerald dropped down after tea, I knew he was dead and I knew who had killed him. Not just Byron. Me as well. I can tell you that Byron never directly admitted to me that he had killed Fitzgerald, or indeed anyone else. But although I saw him only once during the Lord's Test – at my party – he did call me once or twice, sounded most off and tried to get at me. He was, I suppose, already going mad.

Presumably he will be charged with one or all of the murders. Yes, it did dawn on me eventually that he probably killed my own father. But by this time I was probably in as disturbed a condition as Byron. I do remember, though, that Byron, in one of those calls to me, said that batting might become a pleasure again now that Fitzgerald had 'taken one too many'. Yes, that was his exact phrase. I can only assume that Byron, knowing Fitzgerald's habit of pepping himself up towards the end of the day, managed somehow to substitute a quite lethal dose for the pills or solution that Fitzgerald was used to. It obviously hap-pened in the tea interval, perhaps in that little treatment room where Byron, I gather, tried to give *you* the treatment; or it may have been somewhere else in that strange labyrinth, but certainly not in the Australian dressing room. Fitzgerald would have made arrangements to nip away for a moment and give himself a boost. And Byron was more than capable of following up a programme of close observation and calculated risk. That man has great ingenuity.

Again, Byron must have killed Festing. There's no doubt in my mind that Festing's outbursts on fast and dangerous bowling did not conceal at all – although it may have *seemed* to have done – his instinct (way ahead of yours, darling) that Byron was losing his nerve as a batsman. What he failed to detect was Byron's incipient madness. I was the one best placed to see that, yet I did nothing about it. Festing, the former policeman, should have known better than to have played the game on his own. But then, as it turned out, he wasn't the only one.

I don't recall the moment when Byron left the party – he certainly didn't say good night to me – but he left before Festing. It does seem preposterous that Byron had already planned to steal Hunt's car and then use it to run down Festing. But I'm sure that's just what did happen and that Byron afterwards took the incredible risk (though to him it may not have seemed so) of parking the car near the hospital and of sitting waiting in the dark to see who turned up – apart from the police. He must have known that Festing might not be dead for certain. In which case he might have reckoned it was on the cards that you or me, possibly both, might respond to a call from the hospital. He would have had no compunction at this stage in trying to kill either or both of us. The cricket bat on the back seat was a windfall he must have appreciated, but without it he would surely have tried some other method. After that, with both you and Festing still alive, you might have thought that he would have given up, at least for the time being. I really can't see the point of his taking another fantastic risk by killing my father at his home in the middle of the day. Yet it's quite likely he had reached the same conclusions as Festing and was playing the same silly, vain game of going it alone. I did notice Byron and Philip having a fairly long conversation at the party. Byron that night was unusually sober and alert (like the night at Newark) and it's possible that his mad logic convinced him that here was another candidate imperilling his security. Who knows, maybe Philip had asked him to lunch along with you with a view to staging a spectacular confrontation à la Hercule Poirot?

Whatever the truth of that, Byron got there first. Or did he? It still bothers me. This murder seems to have been the oddest and the most outrageous of them all. And isn't it strange that

Byron, after trying to kill you with a cricket bat, put the thing to its true use and played the greatest innings of his life?

Now then (I'm coming to the end, so hang on), don't worry about Polly. She's a pathological liar and a born survivor. She has never once seriously intended to kill herself. I believe they call actions such as hers 'suicide gestures'. That's our Polly. Incidentally she will be without pills for a few days because I found another supply in her room at Kettles and pinched the lot. And Eileen will be all right. She's a dear, good woman, a sort of mother figure where I was concerned, though not my mother alas. I have left her the contents of my flat and the money in my bank. Philip has probably left me a packet. God knows how that will be sorted out. How jolly it was to have money! That will do. I have been spending my capital, like my life, at a very dangerous rate.

I am sorry to leave you in the lurch and I'm sorry we parted so abruptly at Lord's on Tuesday morning, but perhaps it was just as well. I think I found out enough to know that your life is not in danger. That was the main thing. The rest is pretty much silence really. Strange how the rain came too late, or maybe one should say it was perfectly timed, rather like that great catch Byron took in the gully. When the deadly weather comes round again think of me at moments like those.

Good-bye.

Oh my God! Poor Julia! If only I had fancied her less and tried to help her more ... But by now I was through with evasions and showed this letter to Peggy and to Inspector Green. There is little more to tell. After much fuss and speculation Byron, charged with all the murders and the assaults on me, was found unfit to plead. I was thus spared a sensational and harrowing trial in the courtroom but it still pursued me in insidious forms in both public and private life. I refused to write a word on the subject. I never did get to see the Editor, Mr Black. He fired me – and Willie too – but the Sports Editor immediately got another job and I packed up journalism. Green did badly too. There was severe and sustained criticism of his handling of the case. He left the force and took a job as chief security officer for a firm in Bristol. He did tell me that Byron admitted everything apart from the murder of Brooke-Stanley and that if an opportunity arose Byron would like to discuss the matter with me.

Byron is a model prisoner somewhere, with a passion for physical fitness, and no doubt they will set him free one day. Then we shall see. Polly sold her story to a Sunday newspaper and then married a Cheltenham doctor who once had an affair with Dr Stiell's wife, Muriel. I have heard that Polly and Muriel go on holidays together. Wheels within wheels. Meanwhile I am united with my wife and family, living in a new house and doing a different job. I am as happy as can be expected and I must say, against all the odds and to my continuing delight, not only General Quilliam but Forester and all the rest of them still make me welcome at Lord's.

More about Penguins
and Pelicans

Penguinews, which appears every month, contains details of all the new books issued by Penguins as they are published. From time to time it is supplemented by *Penguins in Print*, which is our complete list of almost 5,000 titles.

A specimen copy of *Penguinews* will be sent to you free on request. Please write to Dept EP, Penguin Books Ltd, Harmondsworth, Middlesex, for your copy.

In the U.S.A.: For a complete list of books available from Penguins in the United States write to Dept CS, Penguin Books, 625 Madison Avenue, New York, New York 10022.

In Canada: For a complete list of books available from Penguins in Canada write to Penguin Books Canada Ltd, 2801 John Street, Markham, Ontario L3R 1B4.